WAKING THE SIREN

By

J.E. Taylor

Waking the Siren

Kylee has another mission and a new ally, but will it be enough to battle the desert heat?

Virtue and devotion.

Who would have thought those two qualities could get you killed? When a bicorn terrorizes Las Vegas, that's exactly what this murdering beast targets.

Kylee Paradox is given the mission to bring this monstrosity to justice, but the desert does not bode well for a siren. In fact, it could be just as deadly as the monster she is hunting.

Chapter 1

IT HAD BEEN NEARLY a decade since I slayed my brother, and I was still mute from Fate's punishment. The witch had stolen my siren out of spite, and as I stared over the aquatic scenery from my office window, I wondered if I'd ever get my voice back.

My computer buzzed, interrupting my wandering thoughts. I swiveled the chair around, dismissing the view of the Pacific for my oversized cherry desk. I glanced at the instructions that flashed on the screen, clenching my teeth in response. The next menace on my list was a bicorn. I hadn't run into one of those bastards since the fall of Rome.

It seemed one had come out from hiding and started a killing spree. Culling the virtuous and devoted men of... I stared at the city and let out a silent laugh. What the hell?

Las Vegas?

That was not expected. My fingers poised over the keyboard to question my handler's judgment. The last place I wanted to go was the desert. Besides, everyone knew there was no virtue left in Las Vegas.

I slammed my nails against the proper keys and sent the city with a question mark.

The space between my desk and the door shimmered, and the newly crowned Fate stood before me. This girl was stuck somewhere between teen and adulthood, and she seemed much softer than the bitch who had been on the job since I escaped the binds of hell. But as anyone who encountered me knows, looks can be deceiving. Word on the street was this little young thing was the one who killed the wicked witch.

I still had yet to pass judgment on whether she would follow in her predecessor's footsteps or not. As if she understood my hesitation, she slid a printed instruction paper onto my desk, tapping it for emphasis before she settled in the overstuffed chair.

"Yes. Las Vegas. And this bicorn thing is killing people that aren't on my list. I'm sure you remember the imbalance that occurred the last time someone started reaping those that weren't on the list," she said in her soft, young adult voice that made me want to strangle her for stupidly passing up human existence for this godforsaken joke that was immortality.

I huffed at her. I remembered the catastrophe as well as she did. It caused another breach in Purgatory, which has kept me busier than I cared to admit. At least Fate and Death had a handle on the beast from the inner realm— Leviathan. I'd hate to be the one who had to corral that monster.

I remember, but, really, isn't there anyone else? I signed.

She raised an eyebrow. "Do you see a line of bounty hunters behind me?" She hooked her thumb at the space over her shoulder.

This wisp of Fate was definitely not a pushover.

But it's the desert, I signed. Being that far away from the ocean was bound to create some issues for me. I never strayed that far for very long, and the desert was one place I avoided at all costs.

Fate glanced out the window and sighed. "Lake Mead is nearby, and if you're in a pinch, you can always take a dip in the fountain at the Bellagio."

I stared at her and cocked my head, narrowing my eyes. *It's not the ocean.* My hands moved faster with my agitation.

She sighed. "I know. But you're the only one I have at my disposal."

You've got Leviathan, I signed.

She laughed a full laugh that was both endearing and grating. "Can you see Levi in Las Vegas?"

Okay. She had a point. Leviathan in his true form would likely destroy the city like something out of a bad *Godzilla* film. I slowly shook my head before turning my chair around so I faced the sea.

"Ms. Paradox, I know this is hard," she started.

I glared over my shoulder at her and then twisted my chair so she could see my hands. *It's Kylee, and you have no idea what the desert does to me, do you?* I looked back at the ocean while silence filled the room.

Fate stepped into my line of sight and leaned on the windowsill. She shook her head, and her

4

chocolate eyes softened. She really hadn't been in the position long enough to see what the effects of being land-bound did to me.

Three days. That is all I ever have away from the sea. Seventy-two hours, and then this form breaks down. I waved at the Barbie-doll figure I was cursed with. *It starts with dry skin, which isn't that uncommon away from the water, but the dry skin leads to my hair becoming like corn husks left in the sun too long.*

"Can't you bring moisturizer?" she asked, but it wasn't in the least bit sarcastic. She was honestly thinking human moisturizer would work.

Fate, you really are clueless, aren't you? I signed, wishing for my voice so she could get the nuance of sarcasm.

"First of all, please, call me Julia." She shifted. "Every time I hear the name Fate, I think of that bitch that had this job before me." She shivered and glanced out the window. "And as for being clueless, yeah. I am. In case you hadn't noticed, I'm kind of new here, and the only thing I have about you is the contract you signed." Her gaze swiveled to mine. "But I do know the contract is binding, and I can't change that, even if I wanted to. You will be released when the last creature is returned to where it belongs. So, why don't you enlighten me?" She crossed her arms and raised an eyebrow.

Well, Julia. I paused and met her stark stare. *If I don't get back to the sea by the time five days have passed, I look like a dried up corpse.*

"What happens after five days?" she asked, cocking her head like a puppy.

I don't know. I have never gone beyond five days away from the sea. Five days is brutal enough, and I've never wanted to push that boundary. At that point, it takes me something like three months to recover. But that is under normal conditions, like the Swiss Alps or the Russian tundra or even the Midwest. The desert is an entirely different beast. If I don't find this thing in the first couple of days, the chances of me having the strength to kill it... I clenched my hands and shook my head.

Fate glanced at me and blew a stream of air through her lips. She turned, facing the ocean. Her bottom lip sucked between her teeth as she pondered my words.

There wasn't anything more I could add to the conversation, so I waited for her to speak.

With a nod, she turned towards me. "I need you, Kylee. And not just for this job. You're the only one I have that's bound to bring these things in. So, I guess I have to make sure I get you some solid intel, so you can get in and out before any actual damage happens. We will try to shoot for wrapping this up within three days, okay?"

I blinked and leaned back in the chair. The idea that she was going to help in any way was a new one. The old Fate got off on seeing her patsies suffer just enough to understand who had the upper hand. This girl didn't seem to be the overbearing type at all. Firm, but not nasty.

I nodded. Feeling bold, I asked, *Do you think I can get my voice back before you send me on this job?*

Julia glanced out the window with a sigh before she looked down at the floor.

I waved my hand in her field of view. *Well?*

"I'm not sure how," she finally said after staring at my hands. She met my gaze. "I'm not sure if it's as simple as giving you the vial or not. But we can try when I bring you the instructions, okay?"

Okay. I bit my lip and asked my next question. *Can you tell me how close this will bring me to my salvation?*

Fate pulled out her cell phone and pressed a few buttons before she swiped her finger across the screen multiple times. With a sigh, she said, "There are still a few hundred creatures topside, and unless they go rogue..."

I moved my gaze out to the ocean. A few hundred wasn't insurmountable. It actually was more palatable than not knowing had been, but her last statement really burned. I counted to five to keep my temper in check.

What do you mean 'unless they go rogue?'

"I wasn't planning on hunting them down," she said in a small voice.

So, I'm just stuck here? I balled my hands into fists.

She opened her mouth to reply, and creases appeared in her forehead. Her mouth closed, and she sucked her bottom lip into her mouth, offering me what looked like a consolatory shrug. "If they aren't hurting anyone, I'm not bound to bring them in," she finally said.

And my contract isn't finished until they all are brought in.

She nodded slowly. "Assuming there isn't another breach," she said, scrunching her nose in disgust. "Why would you ever sign such a shitty contract?" she added and pointed at her phone.

I was well aware of the many nuances of that fucking contract. However, this last bit of news grated on my nerves like a desert sandstorm.

I met her gaze. *Because the alternative was worse.*

Fate glanced outside again. "I still would have bartered," she mumbled and slid the phone into her pocket.

I was young and foolish and didn't think I had a choice. In the meantime, can you please figure out how to restore my voice?

The girl nodded. "Let me go get you the intelligence you'll need for this trip. In the meantime, pack and be ready for my instructions." She blinked out, leaving a soft breeze in her wake.

I had a feeling that this new Fate would be more of an ally than her predecessor. I always thought the old one wanted me to fail. That bitch had wanted me back in the confines of hell.

Chapter 2

I STEPPED INTO MY home on Ocean Front Walk and smiled at the orange sky beyond the wall of glass facing the beach. The entire back of my house faced west, so I was blessed with amazing sunsets. Every sunset in progress left me breathless and longing for the days where all I did was swim in the tropics. Of course, those were also the days I lured sailors to their death.

My house was bigger than Alex and I really needed, four bedrooms in a sprawling white setting, but those extra bedrooms came in handy for hiding all my antiquities. I had enough of an arsenal hidden away to be considered a military fort, but these were not the normal military grade weapons. They were the only artillery that could take down supernatural monsters. From simple gemstones that could neutralize garden variety ghosts, all the way to daggers made of stone or wood used to kill beasts from hell.

A bicorn could only be killed with a dagger made of pink ivory wood. I prayed I still had the ones I used all those centuries ago, otherwise I would have to figure out a way to get the wood and make another knife, and there really was no time for that. I turned away from the sun melting into the watery horizon and climbed up the stairs, opting for sweats before I pilfered my artifacts.

After I changed, I descended to the living room and opened the sliders to let the cool sea air filter through my house, recognizing my motions for what they were—procrastination. Rummaging through my weapon store was bound to bring up some unwanted memories, and I was doing everything in my power to avoid going into the third bedroom.

You're being ridiculous, I thought and glanced at the stairwell. My stomach growled, reminding me I needed to eat. I stood at the foot of the stairs, pushing both my dread and my hunger pains away, and trudged up the steps, wishing Alex were home instead of off visiting his kids.

The door to the third bedroom beckoned me, growing in my mind's eye like a funhouse mirror, distorting my vision. I closed my eyes, trying to remember the last time I stepped foot in that room. I shivered. It was the night we got home from killing Jeremiah. Just the thought of his name brought a stabbing pain to my midsection, and I nearly doubled over from the agony.

The hardest job I was ever assigned was taking down my brother. He had gone rogue and was killing sailors off the coast of Greece. Jeremiah wouldn't listen to reason, and my only option was to use my siren. I was always stronger than Jeremiah, and my voice lulled him long enough to pierce his heart with Neptune's trident.

No one should have to kill their kin. The urge to use my siren song died along with my brother, as did some of my inherent caution.

Fate scolded me for breaking the rules, and she reminded me of the price for innocence lost. She reminded me of what was waiting for me in hell. I have not been the same since. Her punishment left me mute, unable to speak, unable to laugh. Unable to ever use my siren again.

Alex noticed my lack of vigilance, too. The last few jobs we were hired for turned out to be more closely aligned with a suicide mission, as opposed to just a run-of-the-mill haunting. We had both been banged up more than either of us cared to admit, but unfortunately, it came with the job. Going up against the supernatural was always a crapshoot, especially without a voice to utter any sort of spell to keep the entity in line. Fortunately, my will to survive had always been strong. I really didn't know how to give up.

Besides, if something happened to me, I wasn't sure what Alex would do. He kept promising me he would break into hell to bust me out, but he was just a frail human who had no idea just how impossible that would be, especially since I was certain he was bound for the pearly gates.

Since my brother died, I had been closer to the breaking point than I had ever been in all the years walking this earth. The rebellion was right there, just under the surface, looking for a reason to break the rules. And my hatred of Fate didn't help quell the need to cry mutiny.

Alex seemed to be the only one who could tame that wild side and keep me grounded. If he had been killed in Greece, or if that witch had seen fit to yank him from my life, I would have already gone off the reservation.

I mulled over the difference between the old Fate and Julia. If the queen bitch had issued the order to go after the bicorn, I would have got my voice back and let loose my siren from the top of the Bellagio just to spite her. The results would have been epic, and just entertaining the idea was almost akin to issuing a dare.

Now that I met Julia in person, I wasn't sure I could betray her in such a spectacular fashion. Especially if that little thing really killed the old Fate. If the rumors were true, then my chances against her would be slim, especially since she was Death's girlfriend.

Enough stalling! I scolded myself and reached for the access panel, stepping in front of the scanners. Once I typed in the access code, a screen opened, and light scanned my face. An unmistakable click followed, and I reached for the doorknob.

Hesitation drew my breath in a sharp inhale as I turned the knob. The room remained the same as the last time Alex and I had stepped inside. My gaze pulled to the long dresser where Neptune's trident was stored, but thankfully I would not have to see the weapon I had used to kill my brother all those years ago.

The dresser was not where my pink ivory wood blades were. Instead of turning toward the bureau, I crossed to the trunk at the foot of the four-poster bed.

Kneeling before the finely crafted trunk, I found the buttons and pressed them in the precise order to unlock the hidden compartment. The click alerted me that my memory was as good as it was the day I set each of the locks. I pushed open the top, and instead of neatly folded linens, the display case of ancient and ornate daggers hidden underneath the blankets was now in full view. I slid the glass aside and picked out the two wooden knives.

"You have a case?"

My heart squeezed. I jumped at the baritone voice behind me. On instinct, I leaped to my feet and spun, nearly launching one of the daggers.

Alex put his hands out. "Whoa there," he said, his eyes wide.

I lowered my arms, but considering my hands were otherwise occupied holding the weapons, I couldn't answer him. I turned back to the trunk and pulled out the sheaths, then slid each blade into its holder before I closed the display case and the trunk, reengaging the locks.

Alex waited patiently for me to lock up my arsenal and followed me into the bedroom. I threw a suitcase on the bed and dropped the knives into it, and then I turned to him. Before I started explaining this new job, I stepped closer and palmed his cheek. Gray circles remained under his eyes, making them darker than normal.

You look tired, I signed.

He offered a half smile and a shrug. "Any time I deal with Mallory, it's exhausting." He caught a gentle kiss.

The way he said his ex-wife's name always came out like he just swallowed bitter medicine. To say he disliked the woman was an understatement, and I couldn't blame him. She had thrown a proverbial shit fit when she found out he had moved on.

The minute Mallory found out Alex was living with me, she tried to get the courts in Los Angeles to take away his visiting rights. I had gone with him to court, and when they realized I was a mute, he gained some sympathy from the judge, and Mallory lost her case. But that didn't mean she would make things easy. She had full custody and his visiting rights were limited to one weekend a month and one week a year, but she made it so the week was when the kids were in school. That meant Alex had to go stay in a hotel to see them. Mallory wouldn't allow them to come to San Diego under any circumstances, and she wouldn't let him see the children if I was around.

For someone who threw the man away like an old pile of trash, she certainly wasn't taking his attachment to me as if she was over him. If I could get away with it, I would gladly go slit her throat. Unfortunately, she was an innocent, and I would be trading my life with Alex for eternity in hell.

The man in front of me would never forgive me for that. As much as he wished her ill will, he also knew she took good care of his children. His tolerance of her was admirable, and another reason I adored him.

"So, a job?" he nodded towards the suitcase.

I nodded and spelled out *Las Vegas* with one hand.

Alex's sexy lips twisted into a smile. It was as if those two words revived him. "So my efforts to get you to a Vegas wedding chapel finally wore you down?"

I rolled my eyes. Alex had made proposing to me an annual event until a couple years ago. At that point, he stepped up his efforts and started asking me almost every month. It was as endearing as it was frustrating. We had been over this so many times, but the light dancing in his tired eyes pulled a sigh from me. I cocked my head and raised my eyebrows in my 'Really?' expression.

"Come on!" He purposely gave me those sweet, wide eyes that I had a very difficult time saying no to. "It'll be fun," he added when I pulled out of his grip.

I shook my head. *This is a job,* I signed. *One that you probably should hang back for.*

"Like you really have a choice," he said.

I crossed my arms. This was the same argument we have had for the last ten years. He knows I'm immortal and can kick ass in any sort of combat situation, but he still insists on putting himself in harm's way just to ease his mind. He thinks he keeps me safe, and in a few of the cases that worked out. But with a bicorn who targets those with high moral virtues? No. Not happening.

Alex, this is as dangerous for you as going after my brother was.

His face fell, as did his arms, and he stared at me. Rightfully so. I hadn't mentioned my brother since the night we got home from that trip and he consoled me on the beach. Neither one of us had mentioned Greece in years, so my bringing it up held weight.

"What are you going after?"

A bicorn, I signed.

He blinked, and his gaze jumped from my hands to my face. "An acorn?" he asked with a crease between his eyes.

All the seriousness of the conversation went out the window. I cracked up. I was laughing at him and he knew it. His face turned red, and an embarrassed smile surfaced, breathing some levity into the evening.

B-I-C-O-R-N, I signed slowly and waited for him to say each letter before continuing to the next.

"What the hell is a bicorn?"

I went to the tablet on my nightstand and typed in the term, scrolling through the search results until I found the most appropriate lore. He scrolled through the text and closed down the screen.

"So, it devours faithful and devoted husbands?"

I nodded.

"We aren't married. Yet." He crossed his arms.

I raised an eyebrow. *It targets faithful and devoted lovers, and unless you've been messing around behind my back, that describes you.*

"And this thing looks like a horse?"

I shook my head. Images from Rome snapped off in my mind. The true form of a bicorn was a hideous display—a faceless two-legged animal with a hole full of razor-sharp teeth in place of a mouth, claws that could shred humans in one swipe, and no eyes to speak of. But they gravitated towards beauty, taking on stunning forms to seduce their victims.

They can take any form they want, I signed.

He stared at my hands, and then his gaze rose to meet mine. Instead of asking more questions, he stepped in and delivered a kiss that stalled my mind.

"I'm going," he whispered as his lips moved to my neck. This was his tactic when he didn't want an argument, and for the most part, it worked. He sidetracked me with his lips and his hands, both caressing and possessive.

This time, however, I pushed away long enough to sign, *No, you're not.*

He acknowledged my hand signals by lifting a single shoulder before moving me to the bed, and from that point on, my hands were otherwise occupied.

Chapter 3

ALEX ROLLED AND PROPPED his head on his hand. He traced lazy circles on my bare stomach. His gaze followed his movement as if he were in some sort of hypnotic trance.

I snapped my fingers to draw his attention. His fawn-brown eyes met mine. A soft smile formed on his lips, and he leaned over, giving me a small peck.

"I love you," he whispered.

I love you, I signed back. God, how I wished I could say those words out loud. Somehow using my hands to say it was not enough.

"Marry me," he said.

The hopeful lilt I was used to wasn't present in his words. It was more of a statement as opposed to a question. I didn't answer him. Instead, I stared at him and sighed. He closed his eyes, rolling away to sit on the edge of the bed and pull on his jeans. He stood, keeping his back to me as he ran his hands through his hair. Every muscle flexed.

"We've been together for ten years. I just don't get why you are so opposed to pledging your heart to me."

He didn't turn around. I knew just by his clipped tone and stress visible on his back that he was pissed. He headed towards the bedroom door. I scrambled out of bed, cutting him off.

Please don't be mad, I signed.

But Alex didn't bother looking at my hands; he just stared me down. He inhaled enough so his chest puffed out, then he shook his head. "I can't deal with this right now." He skirted around me. A few moments later, the slider downstairs opened and shut.

My heart thundered in my chest. In all this time, I had never seen him go silent in his aggravation with me. He had yelled, stomped, cursed up a storm, and even thrown things a couple times, but this quiet anger turned my blood into ice. I pulled clothing on as quickly as possible and sprinted to catch up to him.

He had planted himself at the edge of the surf, letting his feet get wet with each wave. I stepped in front of him, blocking his view of the endless Pacific. He didn't meet my gaze, but the muscle in his jaw tightened.

"Leave me alone right now, Kylee. Otherwise, I might say or do something I'll regret."

The softness of his voice terrified me. I crouched in front of him. *Marriage is a commitment of forever,* I signed. *Your forever and mine are vastly different.*

His eyes narrowed and his jaw clenched. "You keep saying that." His growl matched his glare. "And it pisses me off. I've given you everything, even giving up time with my kids for you, and you can't get past making a commitment?" He made finger quotes as he spat out the word *commitment.* "What makes you think you'll live longer than me, anyway?" He stood and turned north, trudging up the beach, sending small sprays of sand with each step.

I stared after him. *Because that's how it always works out.*

Instead of chasing after him, I left him alone, but it wasn't out of consideration for his wishes. It was out of the raw fear of losing the man. I wasn't sure what would happen when he returned, but I knew if I didn't let him work this out in his head, this would be the end of us.

Didn't he understand that he already had my heart?

I took a seat on the sand and folded my arms on my knees. Water caressed my feet with each wave. The solace I usually found near the ocean was absent. My chest hurt from the weight of his words, and I leaned my forehead on my arms, wondering if I was the one being ridiculous.

"I'll sign a prenup."

I glanced up at him. *What the fuck?*

"You heard me." He crossed his arms.

I climbed to my feet as the burn of his words raked my skin. *You think my hesitation is because of money?*

He shrugged and looked out over the water. "It's the only reason I can see why you won't say yes to me. You're worried I'll bleed you dry."

The fury that filled me was unwarranted, but he knew damned well the money meant zero to me. I wished I could voice the litany of sarcastic responses crossing my mind. Instead, I just lifted my middle finger and spun to head back inside.

His hand clamped down on my upper arm. I reacted and had him on the sand under me with my fist, ready to dole out some justice. I caught myself, uncurling my fist before it did the damage that vicious part of me wanted to do. He didn't even flinch.

"Go ahead," he growled.

No. I went to stand and distance myself, but he again grabbed hold of me.

"You don't give a shit about me," he said through clenched teeth.

All the fire inside fizzled out. *Yes, I do. I just...*

His grip on my arms loosened, and I sat back on the sand.

I glanced out at the dark waters. *Every time I've made a commitment...* I shook my head and folded my hands in my lap. Whether I wanted to admit it to myself or not, I had already committed to him more than I had to anyone else in my lifetime. I knew the real reason I avoided making it legal. The minute I allowed that to happen, this relative bliss would be yanked away from me.

He sat up and hooked his finger under my chin, forcing me to look at him.

"Finish the sentence," he said, but there was no anger there. "Please."

I lose. My vision blurred, and a hot path cut down my cheek. *And I can't lose you.*

His eyes closed, and his chin dropped to his chest. His hand threaded into my hair, and he pulled me into his arms. I buried my face in his shoulder, hating how vulnerable and exposed I felt.

"You won't ever lose me," he whispered in my ear and planted a kiss on my cheek.

His words should have calmed the fear in my soul, but they only made it burn brighter. I would lose him. It might not be for another sixty years, but he would slip away just like all the other humans who had ever become close enough to find the chinks in my armor.

I pulled away. *You can't come on this one with me.* I wiped the tears from my cheeks.

Alex closed his eyes for a moment. When they opened again, a flash of anger hardened his gaze. "Was this all an elaborate ploy?"

I shook my head, stopping him. *I'm afraid.*

A crease appeared between his eyes, and his head cocked.

This wasn't a normal statement coming from me. I had never once admitted to being scared in the entire time I had known him.

"This thing in Las…"

One shake of my head halted the beginning of his assumption. It wasn't the bicorn that scared the shit out of me.

He pointed to his chest, and his eyebrows arched. I slowly nodded.

He broke out in a smile. "I scare you?"

I oscillated my hand back and forth like a see-saw and shrugged. While most of the time I wished for my voice, right now I wasn't sure I could articulate the fear so he would understand. I tried anyway.

What we have together is perfect, but the minute I step into a chapel and profess my love for you in front of God… I curled my hands closed.

"What do you think will happen?"

I didn't want to spell it out. I didn't want to curse what we had.

The air shimmered next to us, and I was relieved that I didn't have to answer him. Instead, we both stared at the vision of the young Fate standing within arm's reach.

I climbed to my feet, and Alex warily followed my lead.

"Who are you?" Alex asked.

"Julia." She extended her hand.

Alex looked at me and I signed *Fate.* His eyebrows rose, and he glanced at Julia again.

"You can't be much older than my daughter." He shook her hand.

"And?" Julia gave him a ghost of a smile, as if waiting for him to say more.

Alex just stared at her.

She turned her attention to me. "I identified a pattern for you. It seems the bicorn is attacking newlyweds, but we haven't been able to figure out if it's because of booking the honeymoon suite at the various hotels, or if it's connected with a chapel."

Julia wasn't telling me anything I didn't already know from my research earlier today.

"The hotels don't have record of any new employees that have started in the last couple of months, but there are a few chapels that have had new employees start in that same time frame." She handed me a piece of paper with the names and addresses of the Las Vegas wedding chapels with new employees. "I have nothing more right now, but if anything comes up, I'll get you the information as soon as I can."

What about my voice?

Julia reached into her pocket and pulled out a vial. She held it out to me. "As I said before, I'm not sure how to reinstate it."

I snatched the glass filled with light out of her hand just in case she was inclined to pull it away. Without so much as a thank you, I pried the cork out and brought the rim of the opening to my lips. I inhaled the contents. Bitter and burning air flowed down my throat. For a moment, I thought she had slipped me a hot chili pepper instead of the essence of my voice.

Instead of pulling the glass away, I forced myself to inhale deeper until the vial was empty. Whatever magic had been sealed in that bottle for ten years passed into my cells, creating heat that nearly drowned me.

Fear as cold as the arctic layered over the heat, and I closed my eyes, pushing it away as I attempted to clear my throat. I opened my eyes and met Alex's wide gaze.

Alex. My lips formed the word, but no sound came out. Nothing but air over my teeth. Whatever had been in that vial couldn't have been my voice.

I snapped my gaze to Fate.

This isn't mine, I signed.

"It was clearly marked as yours." She shifted her weight. "Fate had a lot of little... trinkets, but that vial was in your folder along with your contract."

I stared at her, unsure of how to contain the heat burning in my veins. The sharp bite of fingernails in my palms harnessed the building anger. I slowly unclenched my fists.

"I wasn't sure if there was something else that was needed to restore your voice. There weren't any instructions in the file." She kicked the sand in front of her as she looked out at the water. "I'm sorry," she added.

"What's in this for you?" Alex asked, crossing his arms. His suspicion of the girl came across in his tone and his glare.

Julia turned her gaze to him. "Excuse me?"

"Why are you helping?" he asked, waving at me.

"Because the desert could kill her." She pointed to me. "And she's the only bounty hunter I have at my disposal."

Alex's gaze whipped to mine. "What is she talking about?"

Great. This was just what I needed. I sent a glare at Julia and then signed, *Being away from the ocean for more than a few days isn't good for me. If I'm away too long, well, let's just say it could take months for me to recover.*

"Jesus, Kylee, why the hell didn't you tell me about this?" He ran his hand through his hair and turned away.

"I'm sorry about your voice. If I find out anything more, I'll let you know," Julia said before blinking out.

Instead of addressing Alex, I glanced at the paper and the names of three different chapels in Las Vegas. He scanned the beach before stepping in front of me and plucked the paper out of my hands.

"You are going to explain." It wasn't a request. The hardness in his features had returned.

My skin flushed hot at the order, and I clenched both my hands and my jaw. After counting to five to keep my temper in check, I relaxed. *I can't be away from the ocean for an extended period.*

"Define extended," he snapped.

I've never been away for more than five days, and as I said, it took months to recover from that. Julia was trying to help by getting me some solid intelligence on where this thing might be so I can get in and get out like that. I snapped my fingers. *So there is less of a danger.*

"And when exactly were you going to tell me this?"

I bit my lip and shrugged.

The paper crumpled in his hand. "This isn't going to work." He headed towards the house.

My heart leaped into my throat at his snarled statement. It took me a minute to recover, but then I followed him. He paused before closing the slider, allowing me to step inside before he shut the door.

He tossed the paper onto the counter and grabbed a beer from the refrigerator before meeting my gaze with a blatant glare.

I lifted my hands to speak.

"Don't." He splayed his fingers at me. "Just don't."

I curled my hands to squash the need to apologize, and he drained the entire beer in one long pull. He let out a burp and slammed the bottle down on the counter. Instead of commenting, I headed upstairs to finish packing.

I closed the suitcase and latched it before hauling it off the bed. When I turned, Alex was leaning against the doorjamb with his arms crossed, watching me.

"I'm trying to figure out what I'm going to do with you." He sighed.

I froze in place and stared at him. The fear that raked my skin on the beach was back, and it kept my hand securely around the handle, unable to engage in conversation.

"How many husbands have you lost?" he asked.

I blinked and held up three fingers.

"Right after the weddings?"

I glanced at the floor and shook my head. I raised two fingers and met his gaze. The first died of old age. But the other two times I allowed access to my heart and agreed to be bound in marriage, my husband died almost immediately after the declaration. One within the first week and my second marriage ended violently within hours of our nuptials. All three died in my arms. I couldn't go through that with Alex, not with how incredibly intense our connection was.

"Do you think maybe Fate had something to do with that instead of God?"

I opened my mouth, but nothing came out, so I dropped the suitcase. *I don't know.*

"Doesn't that seem a much more logical explanation than you feeling like you're cursed?" He approached me and stopped within reach. "After all, you have told me dozens of times you thought she got off on your misery. That she wanted you to fail."

Damn his logic. That fear still tugged at my heart, but Alex had a point. I shrugged.

"It makes perfect sense to me."

No matter how logical it seemed, it still didn't calm my nerves. It didn't quell my intuition, which was having a fit among fits. I trusted that little voice in my head more than Alex's shot in the dark. He stepped closer, clouding my thought process.

You are not coming to Las Vegas with me, I signed.

His jaw tightened. "Then you aren't getting the list."

He had never been this difficult before. I put my hand out expectantly.

He tapped his temple. "It's in here. I memorized the names of the chapels before I ate the damn paper."

I took a step back as my eyebrows rose. The shock of his words caught up to my brain, and my jaw clamped closed. *Damn you!*

His lips formed a smile, but it was not friendly.

I pulled my phone from my pocket, but he plucked it from my hands and chucked it across the room, where it smashed against the wall.

"I am going with you, Kylee."

His growl, along with his actions, was sufficient enough to freeze me in place. His glare bordered on dangerous.

I glanced at my shattered phone. I had one other way of contacting Fate, and I picked up my suitcase, bound for my laptop downstairs.

"It's gone," Alex said, as I crossed the threshold into the hallway.

I stopped and turned. *What is?*

"Your computer. You have no way of getting the information you need without me."

I glanced over the railing at the empty kitchen counter and spun in his direction. I wasn't sure whether to call his bluff. Hotels had business centers, but I knew it would take too much time to hack into my private and very secure server to get to my communication tools.

Fate was not on speed dial, and without my hardware, I was cooked.

The thing that burned even more was Alex knew exactly what he was doing.

What. The. Fuck?

"I meant it when I said I was going, but you keep insisting on brushing me off like I can't take care of myself, or you, for that matter. I have learned enough over the last ten years for you to consider me your equal. I'm your damn partner in all this, but every time you get a call for business, you try to bench me. It isn't happening. It's almost as aggravating as your inability to commit to me."

The suitcase dropped with a thud. *Inability to commit?* I waved at the house surrounding us. *I don't call this a damn inability to commit. Just because I don't need a legal document the way you do doesn't mean I am not committed to you. What the hell is wrong with you tonight?* My hands moved in a flurry equal to that of the inferno raging inside me.

He closed the distance and towered over me. "What is wrong with ME? What the fuck is wrong with you?"

Both our chests rose and fell, and the air between us sizzled with hostility.

Pack your fucking bags, I signed, and he blinked. I took a minute to savor the widening of his eyes before I added; *I guess we are going to Las Vegas.*

Chapter 4

ALEX DROVE IN SILENCE with his foot heavy on the gas. When I reached for the radio, he sent a glare in my direction, stopping me from trying to lessen the tension with a little music.

"I'm sorry I broke your phone," he said after an hour on the road.

I kept my hands folded in my lap and gave him a nod. The uncomfortable quiet settled over us again. I started picking at a hangnail to distract myself.

"What if you brought ocean water with you?" he asked, breaking the stillness.

I rolled my hand, prompting him for more because I was unsure of where he was going with his question.

"It's kind of late now, but what if the next time you have to go inland, you bring a couple gallons of seawater with you? Would that help you survive longer away from the ocean?"

What? To drink?

He glanced at my hands and shook his head. "No, to soak in. To heal if need be."

I had never really considered that, but I guess it would be similar to when he filled the life raft with sea water to heal me after my brother died. I shrugged when he looked at me.

"It might be something to try in case we decide to go see the largest ball of twine." His dimple appeared for an instant before it disappeared.

I stared at his profile. I was still pissed off at the crap he pulled on me, but I couldn't help the silly grin that surfaced. Twine. Who thought these things up? I turned towards the window so he wouldn't see my smile.

"So, you think you'll want to go see that someday?"

I glanced back at him. *No.*

His lips toyed with a grin, and he looked back at the road. "No, you don't think it would work, or no to the world's largest ball of twine?"

No to the ball of twine.

"Still mad, huh?"

I nodded my hand in the "yes" motion. I half expected him to tell me he was, too. But to his credit, he kept his mouth shut. Silence engulfed us once again, and I glanced out my window at the clear night sky.

"I don't blame you," he finally said. "I was a bit of an ass."

You think?

He glanced at my hands and snorted. "Yeah. Not my finest moment. First the shit with Mallory, and then all this with you. I just can't seem to win with any of the women in my life right now."

What happened with Mallory? I signed. I knew he looked tired when he got home, but we started talking about the job, and I never asked how his kids were.

"She wants more money. She's using our situation against me." He glanced at me and then back at the road. "She doesn't want the kids exposed to us, especially since we are living in sin. She doesn't want them to think what we are doing is okay, and they are at the age that us living together could affect their morals." Venom filled his voice, and his grip on the steering wheel tightened. "She fed me some bullshit about how her lawyer thinks they have a case."

A slow burn started in the pit of my stomach and I glared at him. *You proposed to me to appease your ex-wife?*

"No, I proposed because I'm in love with you. I'm tired of games and half truths, Ky. I need more, and I don't give a damn that you're immortal and I'm not. I want to marry you because without you, I'm not whole." His grip on the wheel loosened, and he sighed.

"And for the record, I got mad because Mallory got into my head." His bottom lip slid between his teeth. "I don't know what the hell she was thinking, but she made a pass at me."

I remained silent, but my heart picked up and my skin flushed hot. I didn't know whether to be angry or scared, so I let both emotions duke it out.

He glanced at me. "I told her to back the hell off because it would never happen. Not even if she was the last woman on earth."

I exhaled a breath, and the heat faded.

"She then launched into a rant of epic proportions. She sure knows the buttons to push and the things to say that trigger hefty doses of doubt in my mind."

What did she say?

"She said you obviously didn't love me. Not if you weren't willing to marry me."

You told her I didn't want to marry you? I signed.

Alex stared at my hands and then focused on the road. "Yes. When she started hammering me about us living together, I made the mistake of saying that it wasn't my choice that we weren't married right now. And Mallory took that as an open invitation to throw herself at me."

I looked out the window, but his hand slid onto my thigh and gave it a squeeze.

"I got mad because I thought maybe she had a valid point."

I couldn't deal with Mallory and her games. Nor could I make any comment about the murderous thoughts that paraded through my head. Instead, I focused on the more immediate destructive actions of his.

While that explains your explosion on the beach, that does not explain eating the list and destroying my phone and computer.

He chuckled. "Your computer is fine. I just hid it in the oven, which we both know would be the last place on Earth you would look for the damn thing. I said I was sorry about the phone, though." He glanced at me. "You not telling me that being away from the ocean is dangerous didn't help. In fact, it just compounded my doubts along with everything else."

Alex offered me a shrug and shifted his hand onto the console between us. I slid my fingers through his as a peace offering. He closed his hand around mine and squeezed.

"I'm sorry," he whispered.

I squeezed back and focused on the dark outside the window, allowing all the horrifying things I wanted to do to that woman dance through my mind.

"Are you okay?" he asked after a few more minutes of silence.

I met his gaze, nodded, and pulled my hand from his. *Just trying to figure out which weapon in my arsenal would be appropriate to use on Mallory.*

He laughed. "I can only imagine." When his laugh wound down, he said, "You know you can't go after her, right?"

You would get custody of your girls, I signed.

He shook his head. "As much as it would be a relief for us, it would crush my girls, and I could never do that to them."

I know, I signed, but he couldn't stop the decadent fantasy playing in my head.

"You're still imagining stripping her skin off, aren't you?" he said.

I tried to hide the smile that surfaced and looked out the window. His chuckle confirmed he got the message, and I snuck a sideways glance at his handsome profile. He was more beautiful than Achilles had been, and I couldn't blame Mallory for regretting her choices. Alex had become more handsome in the last ten years than that first day I met him.

"I need to grab a coffee before we leave civilization." He pulled off the highway into a gas station. He got out of the car, and I admired his backside as he headed inside the convenience store. He came back with two coffees and handed me one as he took the driver's seat.

"So what hotel are we going to?" he asked and started the car.

Bellagio.

"Nice." He put the car in gear and pulled back onto the highway.

Are we okay? I asked.

He stared out the windshield. "I think so," he finally answered. "I mean, I'm still a little irritated with you, but that's my problem, not yours." He took a sip of his coffee and put it back in the cup holder next to mine. "I'm not going to lie. There is a part of me that wants to cut and run, but my heart won't allow me to walk away."

His words didn't settle my unease; in fact, they compounded it. I was glad when he flipped on the radio and started singing along to the music. His complete lack of tone made me smile. He rested his arm on the console with his fingers inches from his coffee.

I slipped my hand over his, and he gave me a crooked grin. The rest of the drive was filled with soft music and his off-key crooning. It was times like these that I wanted to join in, but even if I had my voice, that would never happen. Not while Alex was by my side. I couldn't condemn him to madness.

Chapter 5

THE WAY THE LIGHTS brightened as we drove closer, intrigued me. I had never been to Las Vegas, and all I knew about this city was what I saw on television and in the movies. The growing glow in the distance captured all of my attention.

"You look like a kid who has just come down the stairs at Christmas," Alex said, breaking the quiet between us.

I grinned and nodded. *I have never been to Las Vegas.*

"You've never been here before?"

No. I try to avoid deserts, remember? I signed.

"Well, then, we need to do this so you get the full effect of the strip." He moved into the right travel lane just as we passed exit thirty-two. He took the next exit, turning right, and then almost immediately took a left onto South Las Vegas Boulevard.

As we passed a golf course, the famous WELCOME TO FABULOUS LAS VEGAS sign stood out against the overload of neon in the distance.

The amount of people out made me both grin at the spectacle and grimace at the task of finding the bicorn in this activity. However, I was thankful this wasn't New York City, where crowds were still milling about long into the wee hours of the morning. By the time we passed the MGM Grand, I cursed silently at both the sensory overload of lights and the increase in the nighttime population. In this part of the strip, it was more like the Big Apple than I cared to see.

Alex shifted in the seat and glanced at the clock. "Did you eat anything earlier?"

I shook my head.

"I didn't either."

I raised my eyebrow.

"The paper didn't count," he muttered and sent a sideways glare. "Want to grab a bite after we check in?"

A smirk played on my lips.

"Food. A bite of food," he said after a quick glance in my direction.

I'm here on a job, not a vacation, I signed.

"We have all day tomorrow to find your bicorn. I'd just like a relaxing meal before we get down to business. Besides, I'm fucking starving."

We could do room service?

"I'd rather go out right now."

I almost detected an eye roll in his tone, but he kept his gaze on the road. His rebuff of spending the night in the hotel with me hurt, and I touched his sleeve. *Did you want me to get separate rooms?*

His gaze lingered. "What do you think?"

An icy shiver found my spine, and I wasn't sure whether he was being coy or an asshole. *I don't know. That's why I'm asking.*

"No, Kylee, I don't want separate rooms. I just need a good meal before we do anything else."

I gave him a nod as he pulled into the Bellagio and parked in the arrival lane. We grabbed our bags from the trunk, and Alex handed the keys to a valet. He took the ticket the kid handed him and started towards the check-in counter. I grabbed his arm and pointed towards the Chairman's Lounge.

The arch of his eyebrows made me smile.

Only the best.

"I guess so." He held the door for me.

We stepped up to the counter, and I started signing. The desk attendant stared blankly at my hands before looking at Alex.

"Kylee Paradox. Penthouse Lakeview," Alex translated.

I rummaged in my purse for my license and the credit card that I had made the reservations under. I handed both my pieces of plastic to the concierge. He typed on the computer before glancing up and handing my cards back.

"Your room is all set, Miss Paradox. Will Mr...." The attendant looked at Alex.

"Mr. Cervas," Alex said.

"Will Mr. Cervas be staying with you?"

I nodded and smiled. I signed three words, and Alex stared at my hands before his gaze rose to mine, registering surprise before he recovered.

"I'm her fiancé," he said, and his voice cracked as the word rolled off his tongue. He coughed and cleared his throat. "Can you tell us where the nearest steak house that's still open might be?"

The concierge glanced at the clock. "STK next door at the Cosmopolitan is still open and serving for another hour. Would you like me to reserve you a table?"

Alex blinked and glanced at me. I gave him a nod.

"That would be perfect."

"I will have a car out front for you in..."

"Fifteen?" Alex said.

"In fifteen minutes." The concierge handed me the room keys and showed us a map of the hotel and where the rooms were, as well as the hotel amenities and casinos. He snapped his fingers, and a bellhop appeared and took our bags.

Alex and I followed the bellhop up to the penthouse suite. Our bags were brought into the bedroom as we took in the strip from the living area. I handed the bellhop a twenty and signed,

Thank you. He gave me a slight bow before he left us to our own devices.

The minute the door closed, Alex said, "Bathroom."

I pointed towards the bedroom, following him, and veered into the bathroom marked HERS. Alex gave a laugh as he stepped into the HIS restroom and closed the door. I relieved myself and splashed water on my face before making my way back to the living room.

Alex stood in front of the window, his hands buried in his pockets. I knew a comment was due based on what I had him tell the desk attendant, but he just turned and gave me a nod.

"Ready?"

I nodded and patted my stomach, which was already making itself known with a low grumbling growl. The minute we stepped outside, a chauffeur opened the town car door for us.

Thank you, I signed.

You are very welcome, Miss Paradox, the chauffeur signed back.

I grinned and glanced at Alex. His lips curved in that bemused smile I was used to as he slid into the seat next to me.

"We both appreciate that you are proficient in sign language, but Kylee isn't deaf. Her hearing is as sharp as a bat's."

"Yes, sir." The chauffeur gave a slight bow and closed the door. When he slid into the driver's seat, he looked back at us. "I understand you are going to STK's next door?"

"Yes, thank you," Alex said.

The drive was no more than a blink, and we were under STK's canopy. The chauffeur rushed to open our door for us. Alex slid out and both he and the driver extended hands to help me from of the car. A girl could get used to this kind of treatment.

I took Alex's hand and gave the driver a conciliatory smile.

"Shall I pick you up in an hour?" he asked and closed the car door.

I think we can walk, but thank you, I signed.

Alex said, "It's a nice night. I think we'll walk if you don't mind." He pulled his wallet out and handed the driver a ten-dollar bill.

"Have a nice evening," the chauffeur said.

We waved and headed inside.

Alex stepped up to the hostess box. "Hello, the concierge over at the Bellagio called in a reservation for us?"

She looked at the paper in front of her. "Miss Paradox and Mr. Cervas?"

"Yes, ma'am." Alex leveled his winning grin at her.

The hostess grabbed two menus and led us into the heart of the restaurant. Considering it was after ten, the place was busier than I anticipated, but the hostess weaved through the tables until she sat us down at a table with a view of the Bellagio fountain. After the hostess poured water and left us alone, Alex glanced at me.

"Fiancé?"

I shrugged. I had initially booked the room on the premise of it being for a wedding night extravagance and that my husband-to-be was meeting me here sometime either tomorrow or the next day. I hadn't expected Alex to be with me. Hell, when I booked, I didn't even know if Alex would be back before I had to go.

It was either that or say you were my father. Which would have been a stretch, don't you think?

He let out a laugh. "Well, I guess thank you for that. But I'm still confused."

I looked at the recent news stories of missing persons here, and most of the recent ones were newlyweds, so that aligns with the list that... I paused because I was hesitant to use the word Fate. *The list you ate. So, when I made the reservations, I made them under the guise that I was getting married in Las Vegas this week.*

Alex bit his lower lip and glanced out at the fountain before sliding his gaze back to me. "What if I hadn't come? What would you have done?"

Nothing. I was planning on being done with this job long before the fictional wedding date and just bailing at that point.

Alex nodded and picked up the menu. "What do you want?"

I glanced through the offerings. Steak with lobster topping and béarnaise sauce sounded divine. I folded my menu and waited until Alex looked up.

"Let me guess. Some sort of steak and lobster combo?"

Six ounce with béarnaise and the hearts of romaine salad to start.

"Do you want any sides?"

I shook my head, and he folded his menu as well. As if that signaled our waitress, she stepped to the table.

"Hello and welcome to STK Las Vegas. My name is Pepper, and I'll be your waitress tonight. Can I get you drinks to start?"

"Actually, we know what we'd like," Alex said. "She will start with your hearts of romaine salad and then have the six-ounce medallion steak, medium, topped with lobster and a side of béarnaise sauce. I will have the same, except make mine a ten ounce." He handed Pepper the menus.

"Anything to drink?"

Alex raised an eyebrow in my direction, and I shrugged and waved for him to make the choice for me.

"A bottle of the house cabernet would be fantastic," he said.

Pepper thanked us and stepped away.

No scotch?

"Cabernet goes better with steak."

The sommelier approached the table with the bottle of wine and poured a splash into Alex's glass. Alex swirled the wine before taking a sip. He closed his eyes, and when they opened, he gave a nod. The sommelier filled our glasses and set the bottle on the table before he took his leave.

Alex lifted his glass. "To us."

I lifted mine and clinked it against his. We both took a sip and then the fountain show began, capturing our attention. The waitress delivered our salads as soon as the show finished.

"So, what does tomorrow look like?" Alex asked as we dug in.

I took a few more bites before I put my fork down to answer his question. *You tell me. You have the places on that paper up here.* I tapped my temple and resumed finishing my salad.

He huffed and shifted in his seat. "This might make tomorrow a little easier." He placed a square velvet box on the table between us.

My fork stopped halfway to my mouth at the sight of the ring box. My gaze jumped to his. His hands folded on the table in front of his empty salad plate, and his eyes held a dare I didn't want to entertain. I slowly resumed eating until the last of the greens were gone.

A busboy came by and cleared both plates.

Against my better judgment, I reached for the box. Alex's hand landed on mine, stopping me.

"You have to say yes before you get to see what is inside."

I pulled my hand away and leaned back in the chair.

"We are going to be visiting wedding chapels tomorrow. Wouldn't it be more believable if you were wearing a ring?" Alex whispered. A smile appeared on his face and he leaned back, his gaze focused on something over my shoulder.

The waitress stepped into view with our plates. "Can I get you anything else?" she asked as her gaze bounced from Alex to me.

I shook my head, still staring at Alex.

"Thank you, this looks fantastic," Alex said. As soon as the waitress was out of hearing range, his smile faded. "I've done the romantic proposals, the begging proposals, along with everything in between. This..." He waved at the box. "This is my ultimatum proposal. Marry me. Tomorrow."

Or what?

"You already know the answer to that." He dug into his meal.

I thought your heart wouldn't let you?

He glanced at my hands and then met my gaze. "I love you, Kylee, and I'd gladly lay my life down for you. But I won't wait by the sidelines anymore. I can't. So if your choice is to say no, then all those fears you confessed on the beach will come true. You will lose me. But it will not be because of some angry god, or some misguided sense that the universe is out to get you. It will be because you chose that path." He pointed his fork at me like a freaky exclamation point and then went back to eating his dinner.

My heart clamored in my chest and sweat broke out on my palms. It was my stomach growl that allowed me to focus on something other than the swirl of emotions accosting me. I allowed my hunger to take precedence and focused on the food in front of me. The box mocked me throughout the meal, making it impossible to enjoy the fine cut of beef. Still, I cleaned the plate.

Alex stared out at the scenery, sipping his wine and waiting. Now that there was no more food on my plate to distract me, I had to face his ultimatum. I had to make a decision. What irked me was he was right. He had bent over backwards and asked me in every conceivable way to marry him. Some of which would have been deemed the perfect proposal in a majority of women's minds, but I was too concerned with Fate striking him down to say yes.

With the change in guard, did I really have a valid fear anymore?

I reached for the box because life without him wasn't a life at all.

Alex's gaze snapped to mine. That distant, hard look he wore from the moment we left San Diego disappeared. His breathing picked up. His lids rapidly blinked, as if he was trying to grasp the meaning of my actions. Tears filled his wide eyes, but they didn't spill over, giving them a bright sheen. Then every muscle in his face relaxed into a smile that could light up the night.

I stopped with the box in front of me, measuring what I wanted to say, but before I could start signing, the waitress popped up at the table.

"Can I interest you in dessert or coffee?" Pepper asked.

"We are all set, thank you," Alex said, but he never lost eye contact with me.

"I'll take this whenever you are ready." She put the leather bill holder on the corner of the table.

As soon as she stepped away, Alex whispered, "I thought..."

I love you enough. I signed in a flurry before I flipped the box open. My hand fluttered to my mouth, covering my dropped jaw. The box had not only a stunning engagement ring, but equally dazzling wedding bands.

It wasn't my matching sapphire studded platinum rings that formed the lump in the back of my throat. It was his wedding band. His steel band had an ocean wave pattern that matched the sapphires in my ring. And the thing that tightened the muscles in my neck and pulled tears to my eyes was the beautifully etched tail coming out of the wave.

"I gather I did okay?"

If I had my voice, the laugh that would have escaped would have been high-pitched and nearly hysterical. Okay. He did more than okay, and when he reached over and plucked the engagement ring from the velvet, I dropped my hand from my mouth and offered the shaking appendage to him.

The ring fit perfectly. I stared at it and then down at the wedding bands. *When?*

He laughed softly. "The week we got back from Greece. And I just finished paying for them last month."

He closed the box and slid it back inside his pocket. Beams of happiness nearly shot out of every single cell. His smile captured his joy.

"Think we can pay for dinner now and get back to that penthouse?"

The light sparkling in his eyes set my insides on fire. *Oh, hell yeah.*

Chapter 6

WE BARELY HAD THE hotel room door closed before he slammed me into the wall, pressing his entire form against me as his lips claimed mine. Before I knew it, he had me on the couch, stripped free of clothing. The man was in ravage mode, and I was so hot I thought I'd flash over.

Our tongues twirled in a sensual dance, and when he pulled away, I wanted to whine. But it was impossible to voice my discontent. The minute his teeth nibbled my ear, my disappointment vanished. His hands slid down my sides, creating a delicious tingle through my skin.

Alex ran his tongue down the line of my neck, and my skin broke out in gooseflesh. I arched into his mouth as he suckled my breast. I ran my fingers through his hair while he went from one nipple to the other, sucking until both were hard and I was wiggling under him.

He knew what I wanted. He played with me, moving lower at a pace that would have made a glacier look like a speedster. I think he licked every inch of my belly in his slow progression south. When he avoided my core and attended to the inside of my thighs instead, I thought I would scream.

God, if only I had a voice.

My eyes rolled back in my head the moment his tongue hit the mark. I arched and silently moaned. Vibrations formed in the back of my throat, and I snapped my mouth closed. The only time I ever felt that sensation was when I used my siren. The shock cooled me to the point I lost track of what Alex was doing.

That was soon rectified as his tongue circled my clit in that way that drove me wild. Whatever thoughts I had fled, and my body drank in every masterful move of his, responding with a rush of wetness every time he hit that magical spot.

When he abandoned the space between my legs, I tightened my grip on his hair. His dark eyes met mine as he worked his way up my body. He paused at my breasts again before his lips found mine. His member filled me with one thrust, knocking the air from my chest.

After the first few thrusts, Alex tempered his pace and took a deep breath. He met my gaze as our hips moved in a slow concert. His grin appeared, and his eyes sparkled with the intensity of the moment.

I mouthed the words; *I love you.*

"I love you, too," he said, his voice a husky growl as he tried to hold on to this a little longer.

His hips sped up, grinding into me in a way that let a tidal wave loose within me. My head tilted back in ecstasy. Alex's eyes clamped shut, and the muscles in his neck and arms tightened. His groan accompanied his release. His eyes opened, meeting my gaze. His jaw tightened with the aftershock that went through both of us, and then he relaxed, nearly collapsing on me.

"I need sleep," he whispered in my ear and kissed my cheek.

I raised an eyebrow. He was usually good for at least two rounds.

He chuckled. "I'm exhausted, babe. I've had one of the worst days of my life and I never thought it would end this way."

I cocked my head. He was familiar enough to know my questioning look.

"I honestly thought with everything that happened with us today you would have told me to shove the ring up my ass." He climbed to his feet and offered me his hand. With little more than a quick look at the clothing carnage spread across the room, he led me into the bedroom.

I glanced at my hand, at the ring he gave me, and the reality tingled through my form. I was getting married tomorrow. Holy shit.

His grip loosened, and he grabbed his toothbrush from his bag and stepped towards his bathroom.

The turndown service had placed fancy chocolates on our pillows. I snatched mine, popping it into my mouth before I headed off to clean my teeth.

With my mouth tingling with the minty taste of toothpaste, I stepped back into the bedroom. Alex was already burrowed under the covers, and he rolled towards me with an exhausted smile.

Are you serious about tomorrow?

His smile faded. "Yes. And unless we find this bicorn, we'll be getting married three times, so you might want to wear something other than those killer heels you packed."

I slid under the covers while his words sank in. I glanced at him and then shifted onto my back. *I need a dress.*

"I need a tux, so that will be the first order of business in the morning." He propped up on his elbow and delivered a quick peck. "Tomorrow night, you can return the favor." He nodded towards the living area of the suite.

Before I could respond, he turned so his back faced me. He was snoring before I figured out how to turn out the lights. I stared at the ceiling, watching the patterns made by the neon of the city below. Thoughts twirled in my head, alternating between getting a wedding dress and taking down the bicorn.

My eyelids grew heavy, and before I knew it, the two themes converged into one giant, strange dream sequence that left me tossing and turning all night.

Chapter 7

SUNSHINE PAINTED THE ROOM. I rolled over to see an empty bed. The clothing I had worn last night was draped over the chaise lounge by the window and Alex was nowhere in sight. I sat up just as he stepped into the room with a breakfast tray.

"I figured a hearty breakfast would get us through today." He set the tray on my lap before hopping over to the other side of the bed and slipping under the covers next to me.

The tray held two plates piled with pancakes, strawberries, and bacon. It was an odd combination and my absolute favorites. He poured syrup over my stack and then did the same with his, and we dug in.

The light fluffy pancake drenched in syrup nearly melted in my mouth. It was like a little slice of heaven before a long and possibly grueling day. I leaned over and gave Alex a peck of a kiss and signed *thank you* before I focused all my attention on clearing my plate.

"I looked up places that rent tuxedos, and there are a few in the area that also rent wedding dresses," Alex said as he wiped his mouth.

I glanced at him for a moment. The thought of renting a dress didn't sit well with me, and I scrunched my nose at him.

"You don't want to rent a dress?"

I shook my head and took my last bite of the delicious breakfast.

"You think you'll find something just like that?" he asked and snapped his fingers, the lilt in his voice echoing the doubt etched in his rugged features.

I gave a wave at my form and raised an eyebrow. He didn't understand women's clothing or the one blessing with this body in this century. I was model-perfect, and most off-the-rack dresses fit like they were made just for me. I had no doubt I would find something suitable. I just had to make sure my blades would fit under the skirt because I was not going into the belly of the beast without protection.

He chuckled. "Go clean up." He nodded towards the bathrooms as he took the empty tray from my lap and put it on his nightstand.

What about you?

"I took a shower after I ordered breakfast." He leaned back on the pillows and grinned, lacing his fingers behind his head. "I'm all clean if you feel the need to delay for some reason."

I gave him a coy smile, and while the offer was tempting, the clock was ticking. Getting sidetracked by morning sex would only lead to another nap, and then half the day would be gone. We had some serious ground to cover before I withered away to a dry husk. If that happened, I wouldn't have a prayer in hell at taking down the bicorn.

Rain check, I signed and grabbed my bag.

"I'm holding you to it!" His words followed me into the bathroom.

The warm water revived me, and by the time I stepped out of the bathroom, I was all primed for a day of success with one knife strapped to my leg and the other to my arm before sliding into my shirt.

I stepped out of the bathroom and smiled at Alex. He had dressed and tried to neaten up the bed while I bathed. His gaze washed over me, and an eyebrow rose.

What? You don't like black? I signed.

"Not on my wedding day," he said. "And certainly not yoga pants and flip-flops. Although, that top is sexy," he added and shoved his wallet into his pocket.

I wasn't exactly planning on getting married. I only brought clothing suited for agility and comfort in this heat. Besides, you're not any fancier. I waved at his casual polo shirt, shorts, and sneakers.

He huffed at me. "Your knife isn't exactly hidden in that, either." He crossed to me and flicked the end of the sheath that poked out of my sleeve.

Knives, I corrected. The sheath on the inside of my thigh was well hidden, even under yoga pants. *Well, depending on what dress I get, you might have to wear this instead of me.* I pointed to the exposed end on my arm.

The creases in his forehead smoothed out, and he took my hand in his. "You have room in your purse for this?" He held out the box with the wedding bands in it.

My chest tightened, but I nodded and opened my pocketbook for him. He dropped the box inside and led me out the door of the hotel room. As much as I loved the man, my internal warning bell sounded as we crossed to the elevator. One glance at the smile playing on his lips, and I shoved the anxiety aside.

A limousine waited for us at the curb, and the driver opened the door as we stepped outside into the sweltering heat. I almost wilted from the dry air, but the inside of the cab was nice and cool.

Alex slid inside and rattled off an address to the driver. I gave him a sideways glance after the door closed and the limo rolled down the driveway.

"You didn't want to rent a dress, so I'm taking you to the best bridal boutique in Las Vegas." He grinned. "I'll drop you off and go get my tuxedo. Do you think you'll be able to find a dress in an hour?"

An hour is plenty of time, I signed. At least I hoped an hour would be enough. This time, I wanted perfection. I didn't want to settle for the first thing that fit.

"You can tell me if that's not enough time," he added.

I think an hour is good as long as they can fit me in. If I have to wait, it might be a little longer.

"I had the concierge make an appointment, so you won't have to wait."

I leaned over and kissed his cheek. *Thank you.*

We pulled up in front of Couture Bride and Alex helped me out, leaving me with a peck on the lips.

"I'll see you in a little while." He shooed me towards the door.

I watched him go and then entered the shop. The girl at the table looked up and smiled.

"Do you have an appointment?" she asked, and I nodded. "Name?"

Kylee, I signed.

She just stared at my hands in that panicked expression of those who don't have a clue. Instead of taking on the bitchy attitude that crept up my spine, I made the motion of a pen. She handed me a pen and paper with that pleasant smile plastered back on her lips. When I handed her the paper, she checked her list and stood.

"Right this way, Miss Paradox. We are expecting you." She led me to a large dressing room with an array of dresses hanging from the racks. "Your fiancé was kind enough to give us your size when he called this morning, so we pulled all the dresses that would allow you to walk out today with the dress of your dreams." She gave me a nod. "Ellie will be right with you. In the meantime, be our guest." She waved to a small table with coffee and finger foods.

Instead of indulging in the sweets, I started looking at the dresses hanging from the racks, quickly ruling out a great deal of them. I found a half dozen that piqued my interest and put them on the empty rack in the corner. When I finished my first inspection of the selections, I unclipped my knife from my arm and dropped the sheath into my purse. I didn't want to catch it on any of the dresses as I held them up one by one in front of the mirror.

I stood in front of the mirror with one of the WToo designer dresses held up to me, and while it was beautiful, I couldn't imagine trying to fight off an enemy in a strapless dress. Begrudgingly, I put the Soliel back on the rack along with one other strapless gown I had chosen from the mix.

Leaving me with four options. Before I could narrow it down any further, a small woman who looked no more than eighteen stepped into the room.

I'm sorry, she signed. *I got tied up with another client.*

That's okay. It gave me a chance to narrow down the choices to these. I waved at the four dresses hanging next to me. All of them had some form of silk and lace with a fitted bodice and an A line skirt that would allow me to be agile as well as hide my dagger without detection. Function was just as important as beauty for me today.

She gave me a smile and signed again.

I put my hand up, stopping her. *I can hear, so if you'd like to speak, that is perfectly fine with me.*

She blushed and glanced at the ground. *I'm deaf,* she finally signed.

I had only encountered a couple of deaf people since I lost my voice, and I never knew how to apologize for my assumption. Here, I would be in the room with this woman for a while. It wasn't like I could make awkward excuses and leave, so I gave her a nod and a smile.

I'm sorry.

It seemed inadequate, especially when she waved her hand at me like swatting away a puff of smoke.

Which one do you want to try on first?

I chose a silky Tolli dress. She asked if I wanted help. I shook my head, and she waved to the dressing room. I stepped inside and she handed me the dress. The moment the curtain closed, I stripped down to my lace underwear and unclipped the knife from my thigh, hiding it in my clothing before I stepped into the dress and pulled the straps over my shoulder, leaving the back open.

I walked out of the dressing room area and pointed to my back. Ellie approached and zipped me up. The dress fit loose and it just didn't have that wow factor. My gaze moved from my image in the mirror to Ellie's. She had that same so-so look that I did until she met my gaze, and then her beaming smile sparked.

It's beautiful, she signed.

Yes. But it isn't the dress.

She gave me a slow, knowing nod and waved towards the select few I chose. I pointed to my back, and she unzipped the silk. I didn't bother with the dressing room. Instead, I dropped the dress, stepped out of it, and handed Ellie the garment to hang back up.

This time I chose the Watters dress. This one had illusion tulle and detailed lace, neither of which felt scratchy against my skin like some of the other dresses. This one was soft and sexy, as well as functional.

The moment I pulled the tulle over my shoulders and the sweetheart neckline molded to my breast, I knew this was the dress. The skirt swayed as I moved in front of the mirror. Ellie stepped behind me without prompting and zipped the back in place. She even went as far as buttoning the top buttons. The dress fit as if it were custom made for my form. I stared at the beauty of it.

Do you have shoes in size eight? I asked as I pulled my gaze away from my reflection.

Ellie nodded. Her gaze scanned me and her eyes reflected awe in the same way mine did. And then she hurried from the room.

I stared at the dress. The detail in the lace was subtle and did not overwhelm the dress like some of the other gowns. It accented the sweetheart neckline. I ran my hands over the fabric, smoothing it out before I combed my fingers through my hair, styling it to fall over one shoulder. The illusion was complete. I grinned like a little girl who had just been given a lollipop bigger than her own head.

The door opened, and Ellie came inside with three shoeboxes and something sparkly in her hand. She crossed and handed me a bedazzled headband. I handed it back with a shake of my head. As perfect as the headband would have been, I didn't want to have anything in my hair that might be used as a weapon.

Ellie set the headband aside and offered me the shoebox instead. I grinned at the name on the box. Paradox. Paradox London Pink Scrumptious, to be specific. The open-toe lace shoes were ideal for the dress I stood in. The fact this sales girl seemed in tune with the perfect accents impressed me. I plucked a shoe from the box and pulled the skirt of the dress high enough so my foot peeked out from under the fabric. Ellie took the shoe from me and crouched down to help me put it on.

Once both shoes were on my feet and the skirt settled back in place, Ellie stepped back and gave me a nod, along with a wide smile.

I love it, I signed, still staring at my reflection. Alex would love it, too.

Did you want to try on the other two dresses before you decide?

I shook my head. I didn't need to go any further. This was the dress I was meant to marry Alex in, and every cell in my body rejoiced with the decision. *No, this is the one. This is just perfect, especially with the shoes.*

Are you planning on wearing the dress out of the shop? She asked.

I bit my lip. As much as I wanted to surprise Alex, I also didn't want to put us in the position of being separated at the chapels today. If I didn't leave with the dress on, I would have to change somewhere, and that made both of us vulnerable.

I nodded. *But I'd like to have you bring my fiancé in here for a more private reveal if you don't mind.*

I don't mind at all. If you'd let me take the dress, I'll go have it pressed while you settle the bill and then we will get you set for your big day.

Taking the dress off actually stung. I didn't want to part with it, but Ellie's kind smile and helpful directions were enough to settle my nerves. I threw on the bathrobe she offered me and grabbed my purse, heading for the front counter to pay for the dress.

Ellie appeared at the counter and handed the cashier the billing slip and another piece of paper. The cashier glanced at the note and smiled up at me as Ellie disappeared.

"Ellie is getting your dress pressed and ready for you, so once we are done here, you may return to the dressing room where she helped you, okay?" she said as her fingers glided along the computer keys. "That will be $3,273 dollars." Her gaze left the screen in front of her and met mine. "How would you like to pay for that?"

I fished in my purse, pulling out my wallet, and handed the cashier my credit card. The entire transaction took less than five minutes, and I was back in the dressing room before Ellie returned. In the time I had gone to pay for the dress, the racks of gowns had been discretely removed, leaving only the mirrors, different seating options, and the reality that the room was much larger than it originally looked.

My clothing still lay heaped on the chair in the dressing area. I exhaled. I had thought no one would come into the room, but at least they didn't touch my clothing. If they had, they were in for a hell of a surprise. I glanced at the bathrobe wrapped around me. The cloth fell to just shy of my knees, which was more than enough fabric to hide my dagger. I quickly strapped the sheath around my thigh and sighed. If Ellie wanted me to put the dress on over my head, I'd have to figure out a creative way to lose the bathrobe without revealing the weapon.

I shoved my clothing into my purse and zipped it up before heading to the coffee and pastries table that had sat untouched since I arrived. I picked up a toothpick and speared a cheese cube. The cheddar square tasted fresh, and I followed it with a small cracker before grabbing a water. I took a seat in one of the overstuffed chairs and waited for Ellie to return.

Chapter 8

I GLANCED AT THE clock. Time had ceased to move since Ellie came back and assisted with getting my wedding dress on. I paced across the floor with the train trailing after me. It had been a little over an hour since Alex dropped me off, and each passing minute amplified the dread in my soul.

Ellie came into the room. *He's here,* she signed and hurried over to me, leading me to the elevated platform in front of the mirrors. She placed me and puffed out the train so it trailed down the step. *Facing the mirror is more dramatic, and you in that dress deserve a dramatic reveal.*

Thank you, I signed and folded my hands in front of me. Taking a deep breath, I gave a nod, and she went to the door and opened it.

Alex stepped inside, looking as handsome as I had ever seen him in a designer-fitted tuxedo. His dark hair was perfectly styled the way I adored, cropped close on the sides, and tall and thick on top. His shoes shined just as much as his eyes.

"Wow."

It was as if his voice triggered my ability to move. I turned and smiled.

"You look like an angel." He held out his hand, and I took it, falling into the hug he offered. "My beautiful angel," he whispered in my ear.

I love you; I signed when he stepped away.

"Come on. Let's go get married." He pulled me towards the door.

I grabbed my pocketbook on the way and gave Ellie a wave as we left the bridal salon.

Alex helped me into the back of the limousine and slid into the seat next to me. He rattled off another address and then glanced at me with that hungry smile.

I waggled my finger at him. *Save those thoughts for tonight.*

Even though I shut off the idea for the moment, I could feel the heat pool in my core at the promise in his gaze. I reached into my purse and pulled out the second dagger.

Alex glanced at it and pulled the blade from the sheath. He opened his jacket and dropped the blade in the inside breast pocket. I raised my eyebrow at him.

"Large pocket protector for a large pocket," he whispered and put my palm on his chest over where he stashed the knife.

My gaze dropped to my hand, and I pushed harder. I couldn't feel the knife.

"I told them it was a tradition for my family and that I needed a jacket that could have an antique letter opener stowed in the pocket in a way that the guests would never know." He gave me a shrug and patted his chest. "They came through."

They certainly did. The fact Alex was protected made those internal alarms inside me quell to a quiet blare instead of the relentless roar they had been all morning.

The limousine pulled into the county clerk's office. I cocked my head.

"Marriage license." He opened the door. He turned and put his hand out to help me from the seat.

I grabbed my wallet out of my purse and then took his hand. Alex had done the paperwork online this morning before I woke and it was all ready for us to pick up. We showed our drivers' licenses and signed our names where the clerk told us. Then we were off with the document that gave us permission to tie the knot.

When the limousine pulled into the Bellagio again, my hands formed the question, *Why?*

"Copies," he whispered and hopped out the door. A few minutes later, he emerged and slid into the back. "Little Church of the West, please," Alex said to the driver.

"Yes, sir," the driver replied.

We pulled up to this lovely old chapel surrounded by greenery, as if it were something from a mountain town in Montana instead of in the middle of the desert. The quaintness of it tickled me, reminding me of some of the ancient places of worship I had seen long ago in southern California.

Alex and I exchanged a glance, and he put out his hand. I went to place my hand in his, and a smirk crossed his lips.

"The rings," he said.

My mouth formed a surprised *O* before I turned and rifled through my purse, pulling the small box out. I handed it to him, and it disappeared into one of his pockets.

"Now you can give me your hand," he said.

Heat filled my cheeks as I climbed out of the limousine after him. The driver tipped his hat.

"I will wait for you in the back parking lot." He nodded towards the hint of asphalt that could be seen beyond the grass.

"Thank you," Alex said, as I signed the same.

He pulled the original wedding certificate out of the inside pocket of his coat and took my hand. I stared at the building, wondering if we were walking towards a new life or our demise.

"Are you okay?"

My gaze moved to his, and I forced a smile.

His eyebrows rose. "That's kind of a scary smile."

I rolled my eyes and pulled my hand from his. *I'm nervous.* It was hard to admit just how unsettled I was, and I couldn't say for sure if it was the act of marrying him or the fact we could be walking into a trap.

"Nervous?"

I nodded and patted his breast pocket. The one holding the blade.

His features smoothed out, and his soft laugh filled the awkward silence. "You're worried about the job, not about marrying me?"

I nodded and the tenseness in his muscles eased, although mine were still as taut as a tightly wound string. His hand landed on my lower back and guided me towards the building in a patient but firm manner.

"Relax and enjoy the moment. We'll deal with the monster later," he whispered and opened the door for me.

I stepped inside, and my radar went up. Each face I looked at could be the bicorn. I tried to recall how I flushed the last one out. It hadn't been easy, but I had the luxury of time since I was so near the shore. However, one thing I remembered was the thing had taken on the most stunning female form, almost as beautiful as the goddess Venus herself. As I glanced around the lobby, none of the faces I saw fell into the stunning category. Cute and pretty, yes, but drop-dead beauty wasn't among them.

Would the thing be that cunning?

My brain grappled with that and I finally ruled it out as the receptionist turned her attention to us. Run of the mill cute or pretty wouldn't make a virtuous man crumble.

"Hello," Alex stated. "I called this morning."

The receptionist, whose nametag announced her as Karen, glanced at the list in her hand. "Mr. Cervas?"

"That's correct," he answered and handed Karen the original marriage certificate we filled out at the town hall.

"Right this way, sir. We are almost set for you two." She smiled at me and added, "You are stunning in that dress."

Thank you, I signed with a smile.

Karen led us to the entrance of the small chapel and had us wait to make sure things were ready.

You called?

"Yes. Most places you can't just walk in and get hitched anymore. So we have reservations, like at a fine restaurant." He made finger quotes around the word reservations and winked at me.

So who is the newest... I stopped as the doors swung open.

Karen smiled and stepped out of the way as the music started. I immediately recognized "Just the Way You Are" by Bruno Mars, which was the song Alex always sang to me whenever I was down. I loved his off-key version. This specific detail made me smile.

He tugged me forward. I fell into step with him as we crossed the distance between the doors and the altar, where a pastor waited for us.

Karen handed the pastor the paper and stepped to the side next to a photographer, who snapped a picture of us. He lowered the camera as the pastor cleared his throat.

"Dearly beloved, we are here in the sight of God to join Alejandro and Kylee in holy matrimony. Marriage is an honorable estate, not to be entered into lightly but thoughtfully and reverently." He looked at the paper in his hand and then back at Alex. "Alejandro, will you have this woman to be your lawful wedded wife? Will you love her and comfort her, honor and keep her in sickness and in health, and forsake all others as long as you both shall live?"

"I do."

The pastor turned to me. "Kylee, will you have this man to be your lawful wedded husband? Will you love him and comfort him, honor and keep him in sickness and in health? And forsake all others as long as you both shall live?"

I do, I signed.

He glanced at Karen. She gave him a nod.

"Do you have the rings?"

Alex pulled the box out of his pocket and handed it to the pastor. The pastor opened the box and handed Alex my ring.

"Please repeat after me," he said.

Alex slid the ring on my finger and recited our vows. "I, Alejandro, take you, Kylee, to be my wife. I promise to be true to you, in good times and in bad, in sickness and in health, and I will love and honor you as long as we both shall live. Please accept this ring as a token of my love and fidelity."

I took the ring and slid it on Alex's finger and followed the pastor's directions in sign language. *I, Kylee, take you, Alejandro, to be my husband. I promise to be true to you, in good times and in bad, in sickness and in health, and I will love and honor you as long as we both shall live. Please accept this ring as a token of my love and fidelity.*

After he received another nod from Karen, he continued, "Those whom God hath joined together, let no man put asunder. We who have come together today have heard the willingness of Alejandro and Kylee to be joined in marriage. You have come of your own free will and, in our presence, have declared your love and commitment to each other. You have given and received a ring as a symbol of your promises. Therefore, by the power vested in me by the laws of the state of Nevada, I take great pride and pleasure as I declare you husband and wife. You may kiss your bride."

Alex leaned in and pressed his lips to mine as the music started again. The magical moment was interrupted by the flash of a camera. Alex pulled away from me and grinned. Another flash captured the moment, and we turned towards the photographer for another handful of pictures as the pastor and Karen signed our certificate. The photographer stopped long enough to sign as our second witness before we were escorted out of the chapel.

Karen led us to the reception desk and handed Alex a card with website directions to access digital copies of the photographs. She made each of us sign the certificate again, and then she stamped it with a seal.

"Would you like us to file this for you?"

Alex glanced at me and then nodded. "Yes, please."

"Your photographs will be ready for viewing in just a moment. You are welcome to have a glass of champagne while you wait." She waved towards a seating nook with a fresh bottle of champagne and two glasses. A monitor sat just beyond the bubbly.

"Thank you, Karen." Alex led me away. "You were going to ask who was the latest hire?" he whispered in my ear.

I nodded.

"Karen is their newest employee. She's been here for about a month," he said as he poured two glasses and handed me one. "To us," he added and tapped his glass against mine.

I raised my glass and then took a sip. My gaze moved beyond Alex. Karen was busy with paperwork and never glanced our way. Instead, she focused on the next bride and groom who had been waiting for us to finish.

"Do you think it's her?"

I shook my head. Alex studied me and I shrugged. *Think stunning, not mousy cute.*

A smirk formed on his lips. "Kind of like you?"

Heat filled my cheeks, but before I could answer, the photographer stepped into our nook.

"Hello, Mr. and Mrs. Cervas." He extended his hand to us. "I'm Mark. Your photographs are available for viewing." He reached over the table and turned the monitor on. "Your wedding package includes a wedding album with a dozen photos. As we go through them, please let me know which ones to mark. Additional pages cost one hundred dollars each, so keep that in mind." He smiled and started clicking through the pictures.

I didn't realize how many he had taken in the short time we were in the chapel and by the time we were done, we had it narrowed down to twenty photos. My favorite was Alex's grin after he kissed me. The man's eyes sparkled even on film. We forked over the money for the album and arranged for it to be delivered to the hotel later in the day.

Alex wrapped his arm around my waist and led me out of the chapel to our waiting limousine. When he slid into the seat next to me, he took my face in his hands and planted a lingering kiss.

"Back to the hotel?" the driver asked when Alex pulled away.

"No." He glanced at his watch. "We need to get to the Wee White Wedding Chapel, please."

The driver's brow creased.

"We didn't like what they offered here. We're looking for something a little more... unique," Alex said. "Besides, we have a reservation at two. If we don't like that one, then we have one later this evening as well."

"Yes, sir." The driver pulled out of the parking lot.

A few minutes later, we pulled into the Wee White Wedding Chapel. Alex held his hand out as the driver came around to open the door.

"The ring," he whispered as he slid his off and dropped it into his pocket.

I took it off at his direction with a little more than a pang in my heart, but we couldn't exactly walk in wearing the rings and pull off the getting married thing. Not if we truly wanted to catch the bicorn.

My ring disappeared into the same pocket as his, and he pulled out one copy of the marriage certificate and took my hand. The moment we stepped inside, I knew the bicorn wouldn't be party to the chaos inside. There were several chapels and another dozen brides and grooms standing around, waiting. The staff rushed from one to the next, and it did not give anyone the time to make an impression. Besides, there was not one stunning woman in the lot.

Still, we waited in line until we stood before the desk.

"Name?" the middle-aged woman at the counter said around a mouthful of chewing gum. She was possibly the most repelling creature I had seen in a while.

"Oh, hell no." Alex turned me around, marching towards the door.

I glanced around one last time before we stepped into the sunshine and oppressive midday heat.

What?

"The receptionist was the newest employee," he said as we marched to the limousine.

I actually snorted, surprising both of us, but the silent laugh pushed more air through the back of my nose than I expected. *Yeah, if the bicorn was hiding in that form, it would be starving by now.*

Alex burst out laughing. "No shit." He opened the door for me and climbed inside after I was situated.

"That leaves us with the Vegas Wedding Experience, but we have the rest of the day to relax. They could only fit us in tonight just before they close."

I waved at the dress.

"We could go back to the hotel, where we can both get comfortable," he said with a grin.

"Back to the hotel?" the driver asked.

"Yes, please," Alex answered. "We will need a ride tonight to the Vegas Wedding Experience, though."

"That's a nice venue. They offer a limo service as well. Would you like the concierge to arrange it for you?" the driver asked and focused on the road.

Alex glanced at me and I shrugged. "Sure," he said. "That would be great."

Do you think the spa could fit me in for a mani-pedi and possibly hair and makeup? I signed and pointed to the driver.

"My w…" Alex faltered and corrected himself. "My fiancé wants to know if the spa at the hotel has a slot for her to get a manicure and pedicure along with her hair before we go to the chapel tonight."

"Let me check." The driver called into the hotel. "Does a four o'clock appointment work for you, Miss Paradox?"

Four is perfect.

"She said that is perfect."

I leaned back in the seat and closed my eyes for the remainder of the ride.

Chapter 9

THE MOMENT WE STEPPED into the hotel room, Alex reached for me. I batted his hand away. *We are not going to ruin this dress. Not if we are going to get hitched again tonight.*

"You are my wife right now." He wrapped his arm around my waist and pulled me against him. "And I want to make that official," he purred in my ear.

I rolled out of his arms and turned, pulling my hair to the side so he could unzip the dress. I glanced over my shoulder at him and raised an eyebrow.

Alex slowly unzipped the back of my dress like he was unwrapping a china doll. I appreciated his delicate touch just as much as his care in folding the dress over the chaise lounge. His tux was folded with care as well, and then he faced me. His boxers were already tented with his desire.

His gaze flowed down my body, stopping at the sheath on my leg before continuing on.

I reached to unclasp it.

"No, leave it on." He moved in front of me. "It's fucking hot."

Kinky, I signed.

He grinned and pushed me back on the bed, relieving me of my lace panties before he filled me with one hard thrust.

"I have been waiting to do this since I laid eyes on you in that dress." He closed his eyes and slowed down his pace with a sigh.

I moved with him at that insanely slow pace that drove me wild, especially with the way his pelvis ground against mine. Making love to Alex was always a spiritual adventure—from the decadent and kinky to the sweet like right now, he knew how to make me lose my mind.

He leaned forward, claiming my mouth in a heated kiss. His hips matched the pace of his tongue, lingering at first but then increasing into a wild frenzy that ended with a groan as my nails raked his back with my release.

The kiss broke, and he stared down at me with a sleepy smile. "I love you, my dear wife."

I smiled and gave him a peck. My stomach growled, and I looked at the clock on the nightstand. I didn't have enough time for room service before my salon appointment.

Alex glanced at the space between us. "And here I thought *my* stomach was loud." He rolled away, stretching out next to me.

I took him in, and my smile widened. This exquisite man lying next to me was my husband. The reality hit like a tidal wave, and my vision blurred. I blinked back the heat pooling in my eyes and sat up before Alex caught the tears. I crossed to my suitcase, looking for anything that would be appropriate for a pedicure and still hide the knife from view. Nothing fit the bill, but then I remembered the yoga pants stuffed in my pocketbook.

"What are you doing?"

I waved at my naked body and wiggled my fingers, hoping he would get what I was saying.

"You still have a little time," he said with a grin.

Instead of turning, I headed to the bathroom and relieved myself. I also took a minute to splash cold water on my face to wash away the tear stains. With my emotions in check, I walked back into the bedroom.

Where's my pocketbook?

"In the other room. Why?"

Yoga pants for the pedicure, I signed and crossed into the other room. My purse was on the coffee table. I grabbed both the pants and shirt and headed back to the bedroom.

Alex was still sprawled out on the bed with his hands behind his head. He watched as I picked up our discarded underwear and dropped it on our formal wear.

"Going commando?" he asked.

I shrugged and pulled the pants on over my bare ass.

He propped himself on his elbow. "I think we should do that tonight."

I laughed at him. *Seriously?*

"Yes." He grinned.

I sucked my lip between my teeth as I considered it. *Okay.* I slid my top over my head and gave him a smile. After grabbing my flip-flops and purse, I blew him a kiss and headed out of the hotel room.

Chapter 10

The spa employees at the Bellagio certainly knew their way around pampering a woman. From the relaxing foot soak to the deep tissue massage on my calves, I thought I had entered nirvana, but then came the hot towel wraps and green tea lotion for an invigorating end to the pedicure foreplay.

The chair I sat in had those slow massage knobs that climbed up my back to my shoulders in hypnotizing circles before returning to my lower back. The endless loop left me feeling more like silly putty than a bride. I chose a blood-red nail polish for both my toenails and fingernails. I figured I was already married, and tonight's follies were more for show, anyway.

As soon as the nail pampering was over, I was escorted into the hair salon where the hairdresser put my hair in a braided cascading up-do that put the bridal magazine pictures to shame. I stood in front of the mirror looking at the thick but loosely braided cords at the sides of my head that lead to the web of beautiful curls tickling the nape of my neck. It was gorgeous.

I was pleased, and my monetary tips showed it. When I walked into the hotel room, Alex looked up from the couch, and his eyes widened, almost like they did when he saw me in the dress for the first time. He put down the book he was looking at and stood. He looked fine standing there in just the tuxedo shirt and pants. The jacket lay neatly across the couch next to him.

I blew him a kiss and headed towards the bedroom to get dressed. I didn't have much time left before we had to be on our way. Instead of pulling the shirt off over my head, I stretched it over my shoulders and down my body, stripping the yoga pants with it. The shoes came first, and I buckled the lace sandals before I stood and picked up the dress. The hard part came when I tried to zip it up. I only had the reach to get it to the middle of my back. I needed Alex and crossed to the living room.

He turned towards me when I tapped the wall. I pointed over my shoulder before signing, *Can you zip me up?*

His lips formed the perfect smile. "I didn't think it was possible, but you look even more beautiful than you did this morning." His pants tented, and he shifted as he crossed to me. A blush crept into his cheeks.

I raised an eyebrow at him before he stepped behind me. I swear the man could be as bad as a teenage boy standing in a stiff wind.

"Commando has its drawbacks," he muttered and tugged gently at my zipper until it reached the top of the dress. "The photo album from this morning came." He pointed towards the table. "Want to see?"

Do we have time?

"Just enough for you to at least take a quick look." He handed the album to me before he slid his coat on.

I flipped open to the first page, and my chest squeezed enough for my breath to draw in. Alex's grin captured my heart, and having this memorialized struck a chord deep inside me, bringing those alarms to the surface and ruining the relaxation the last two hours had created in my muscles. Doubt crept in, and a part of me wanted to grab him and hop in the car to head home, where I knew he would be safe.

I looked up at him, and that spectacular smile graced his lips, melting my resolve even further. I knew if I continued to flip through the photos and let these emotions take control; I was going to back out of this job.

And I didn't have the autonomy to do that. I closed the book and placed it on the table, trying to shake the dread clawing at my insides.

I'll look at them later. Let's go before I change my mind.

His smile faded, and he stepped close. "It's a little too late for that."

I rolled my eyes and palmed his cheek, slowly running my thumb across his lips. The desperate need to run from this desert oasis filled every cell. I leaned in, catching a quick kiss before I heeded my own internal alarms.

Let's go catch this bitch so we can go home, I signed as I stepped away.

His cheeks flared. "I thought you meant you changed your mind about marrying me." He let out a small chuckle. "I really need to stop assuming you mean me when you say shit like that."

Yes. You do. I gave him a smile and took his hand.

Alex checked the pocket of his coat for the hotel key before we stepped out of the room, and I gave his breast pocket a pat as well.

"It's there. That's the first thing I made sure of when I put the jacket on," he said as the elevator opened. "And the rings are safely tucked away, too. I think I want the photo package from tonight, as well," he added.

I shrugged. I didn't care. The photo album sitting in the hotel room was enough for me, but if he wanted pictures of me with my hair all decked out, I didn't have a problem with that. As a matter of fact, it was downright sweet.

Okay. I smiled as we stepped into the lobby.

Heads turned as we crossed to the entry. A town car with the wedding venue logo plastered on the side was already waiting for us outside.

"Mr. Cervas?" the driver asked as we approached. There was something vacant in his gaze, but it could be just the end of a long day.

"Yes," Alex confirmed.

The chauffeur for Vegas Wedding Experience opened the door to the back of the town car for us. Alex helped me inside before taking the seat next to me.

I really didn't want to be in the car going towards danger, but then again, if this didn't pan out, we would only have one more day before my body broke down. The caviar hair treatment I received at the spa actually rejuvenated my hair, but that had nothing to do with the fish eggs and everything to do with the fact they stored the delicacy in sea water.

The slow pattern of Alex's thumb on the side of my hand pulled my attention back to the moment. He watched the passing scenery with an expression I couldn't read. I squeezed his hand, and he glanced my way with a smile that held tension at the corners of his lips.

I wasn't the only one on edge. I squeezed his hand harder.

"I'm good," he whispered. "Just nervous that this place isn't going to be everything we want," he added and brought my hand to his lips. His gaze traveled to the driver and back to me.

So I wasn't the only one who caught the weird vibe of nothingness from our driver. He looked pleasant enough, but there was no personality there. Unlike the chauffeurs at the hotel, who all seemed to be talkative and jovial.

I pulled my hand out of his and signed, *Did you remember the wedding license?*

Alex snorted a laugh. "Yes. I have the license and the rings. I have everything we need, so just relax, hon."

"She doesn't speak?" The driver's gaze locked with mine through the rearview mirror for a moment before traveling to Alex's.

"No. She can't speak," he said in a clipped tone that was neither friendly nor welcoming to encourage any more conversation.

"You must really love her to marry a deaf-mute," he muttered from the front seat.

"She isn't deaf," Alex clarified with a hard edge in his voice.

The driver's eyes never changed as he glanced at the two of us. No remorse or surprise at Alex's comment. Even his mumbled apology lacked emotion and sincerity.

My spine tingled with warnings. I wished Alex had had the hotel service take us to this wedding venue instead of using their service. We were heading into the devil's lair without an escape plan.

Chapter 11

WALKING INTO THE VEGAS Wedding Experience lobby wasn't anything I was prepared for. Unlike the bustle of the last place we stepped inside, this one was almost too formal for my tastes. Add to that the fact that everyone working in the place could have landed a modeling job on the spot.

I traded a glance with Alex. He wore the same expression I envisioned on my face. Both of us were overwhelmed.

A petite woman with glasses and an appointment book approached us with a smile. "Mr. Cervas, I presume?" she asked and extended her hand.

Alex shook it and gave a nod.

"I am Beverly. We spoke on the phone this morning. We have you all set for the sunset ceremony. If you will follow me." She led us to the right. We crossed through an empty ballroom and out onto a terrace over a secluded lake. "Martin is all set over at the gazebo and ready to officiate the ceremony. So is Shea, our photographer, who will discuss photo packages with you after the wedding. And Justin is all set to take you back to your hotel after you wrap up with Shea. Now, you also mentioned you would need witnesses?"

"Yes, and at least one of them needs to read sign language," Alex said.

"Yes, that is outlined in the notes here, and I am well versed in multiple languages, including sign language." Beverly smiled up at us and put her hand out. "The license?"

Alex pulled the last copy out of his pocket and handed it over.

I was too preoccupied with the scenery to pay close attention to what the two of them were discussing. The gazebo faced west, and the sun had dipped enough to be visible between two mountain peaks in the distance, reflecting a bright orange path on the water leading to the wedding altar. The sky had turned deep blue with the clouds colored in pinks and purples stretching towards us. It was magnificent.

And distracting. The beauty of this place was hypnotizing.

While Beverly was pretty, the photographer standing with the preacher landed in that stunning realm that worried me.

How long has the photographer worked here? I signed.

"She's only been here a little under a month, but I can assure you her resume and portfolio are impeccable."

I nodded and offered what I hoped was a sincere smile. Beverly led us to the gazebo, and as soon as we stepped onto the path leading up to the outdoor altar, soft music piped through the speakers. The sun dipped lower on the horizon. Everything about this magical situation was wrong. The place was too perfect, too staged, and it was the ideal hiding spot for a bicorn. I glanced at Alex.

He sensed me gazing up at him and glanced my way. "I love you," he whispered as we walked into the monster's lair.

The ceremony was almost word for word as our actual wedding ceremony this morning, but much more surreal with the sun setting behind the officiant. I let my guard down, and when Alex kissed me, I let the kiss linger, melting into him and forgetting for a moment that we stood in the presence of danger.

When the kiss broke, we stared at each other and smiled. The click of the camera pulled us out of the moment. A moment I did not want to end because as soon as we stepped away from this altar, we were back in hunting mode.

Alex seemed to sense my hesitation and wrapped his arms around me in a hug. He twirled me around in a circle and set me on my feet again with a laugh. The sparkle that appeared in his eyes gave me an indication of what type of thoughts were parading through his head, but with another snap of the shutter, his demeanor subdued.

"Are we all set?" he asked, glancing at Beverly and the clergyman.

"We just need your signatures," Beverly said.

We crossed to the podium at the side where our certificate lay. Beverly and Justin, our driver from earlier, had already signed as witnesses, and we signed our names as well.

"I'll make sure this gets filed with the county clerk in the morning," Beverly said as she took the form. "I'll leave you in the trusted care of Shea, who will walk you through the photo packages and see to it you get the perfect representation of your special day."

She shook both our hands. "Congratulations," she added before she strolled towards the main ballroom.

We turned towards Shea.

"Mr. and Mrs. Cervas, congratulations. It has been a pleasure photographing your special occasion this evening. If you will come this way, I can upload the pictures for your viewing and go through the various packages we offer."

Even her syrupy voice grated on my nerves. I shook her hand first, and her face tensed a fraction when her fingers wrapped around mine. It was so quick that I almost didn't catch it. With Alex, she held his hand a few moments longer than necessary, and a spark twinkled in her eye.

Distracted by the nearness of our most likely candidate for the bicorn, I had to still my need to rip the knife from my sheath and bury it in the monster's evil heart. There were still people around, still receptions occurring in the other area of the building. I couldn't do this in public, not if I hoped to get out of here without being arrested.

I traded a glance with Alex, and he gave me a wink.

"We'll take all of them, please," he said as we shuffled through the photos. They were just as gorgeous as the ones in the album back at the hotel, but these had the mountain sunset as a backdrop. "Digital copies," he clarified. "With the release to print at our leisure."

Shea beamed and took Alex's credit card, disappearing into the office.

Justin gave us a nod and headed out of the lobby.

Shea came back with our card and the receipt, along with a card that had instructions on how to download the files.

"I will upload these to the website on the card tonight. I just want to warn you, you will need to download them within thirty days or there is an added charge for reloading them to the website," Shea cautioned and stapled the receipt to the instructions.

"Thank you." Alex folded the receipt, slipping it into his coat pocket before he replaced his credit card in his wallet.

She shook our hands. "I believe the town car should be waiting up front for you. It has been a pleasure," she said and then disappeared, leaving us alone in the lobby.

Alex went to say something, but I shook my head. I took his hand, and we headed out to the car.

Justin stood holding the door of a different, bigger car. This time, he wore a smile that seemed much warmer than earlier. The cab had a single leather bench seat across the back and a stocked bar on the side behind the driver's seat. A privacy shield separated the driving cab from the back as well. It was almost akin to a mini limo. In the middle of the bar sat an uncorked bottle of champagne with two champagne flutes.

"Would you like me to do the honors, sir?" Justin asked after we settled in the car.

Alex glanced at the bottle and then at Justin. "I think I've got it."

"Very well, sir." He closed the door.

The minute the car engine started, the door locks engaged. Alex was too busy prying the cork from the bottle to notice. With the cork safely out, he poured us each a glass.

"To us," he said. "May we have a long and happy life together."

We tapped the glasses and took a sip. I didn't detect any odd taste in the bubbly. Apparently, neither did Alex because he downed the glass and set it aside.

He went to take my still half-full flute, but I pulled it away, finishing it before relinquishing the glass to him. Without a hint of caution, he tossed the cup onto the counter and took my face in his hands.

"I love you, Kylee Cervas." Then he crushed my lips in a kiss that promised all sorts of naughty things when we got back to the hotel.

If I wasn't so pre-occupied about catching the bicorn, I would have melted under it.

A wave of dizziness hit me, and I pulled away from him. He blinked at me, and his forehead wrinkled quizzically.

"Ky..." he started, but never finished. His eyes rolled up into his head, and he slumped in the seat next to me.

The soft hiss coming from the air conditioning ducts caught my attention just before the blackness took hold of me.

LITTLE BY LITTLE, LIGHT bled into my consciousness. Whispers came and went, but I couldn't make out the words. The fog clouding my brain cleared, but my body was still too heavy to listen to my commands to move. My last memory in the limousine snapped my eyes open and catapulted me to my feet.

The only fixture my gaze locked on in this bland room was the large window a few feet in front of me. Alex was on the other side of the glass, tied to a chair, still wearing his tuxedo. His head lolled to the side, and his mouth hung open in a stupor, but he didn't look like he had been harmed.

My heart slammed against the walls of my chest. I went to step towards him. A yank on my arms brought reality to the forefront. Both wrists were bound in rope and anchored to metal hooks on the floor. I couldn't reach the window, even if I strained forward. I tried kicking out in front of me, but it was just too far. The burn of frustration flushed my skin, and I silently cursed.

I glanced around at my surroundings, looking for anything that might aid in my escape, but there was nothing within my reach. Even the table at the back of the room wasn't accessible. The tools on the table froze me in place. It looked like Lucifer's torture chamber had been moved topside. Ropes, whips, knives, and even some horrific toys meant to tear someone apart from the inside out lay organized on the table.

Silence overrode my senses. The door opened. Four men, including our driver Justin, stepped into the room. Their empty smiles mimicked each other, and I shivered, trying to dredge up the facts of exactly what the bicorn did to their female victims. If the table behind me was any indication, I was in for some serious pain.

Men were left as vacant, shriveled shells, the life sucked out of them and their soul. Their soul fed the damn beast, dying just as surely as the bodies the monster left behind.

I wished to hell we had driven ourselves to the venue.

Shock as strong as an electrical current flowed through my form as a woman crossed into the room behind the four men. I blinked and my eyebrows rose. She was not who I expected.

Beverly, the petite wedding planner from the Vegas Wedding Experience, chuckled at me as she crossed the space, holding the sheath that had been strapped to my thigh. She stopped less than a foot away, pointing the leather at me. "I never expected to find this on you," she said, her voice harsher than the one she used at the venue. "Where did you get it?"

I shrugged. With my hands bound, my ability to communicate was stunted. I had to keep up the pretense as long as possible to give Alex a fighting chance. If he woke as groggily as I had, this bitch could easily throw him off his game.

She hissed at me.

I mouthed, *Something old.*

Her eyes narrowed at me. "Did you just say 'something old?'"

I nodded. *Family heirloom.*

"Really?" Sarcasm laced her voice, and she turned to the closest minion. "Handkerchief," she ordered and put out her hand. He obliged, and she wrapped the cloth around the hilt of the weapon, pulling it from the sheath. The leather fell to the floor. Her free hand cupped my cheek. "You really expect me to believe that crap?"

Before my eyes, Beverly changed to my mirror image. Horror filled every cell, and with it came a blinding pain searing my side. I couldn't even cry out as the knife pierced through my insides. Both devastation and fury filled me. She was close enough to me to take the only opportunity I had at my disposal. I head butted the bitch.

The impact left me woozy, but it was worth it. My mirror image stumbled back, yanking the blade from my side. Her dainty nose was twisted at a broken angle, and blood dripped down the front of the image of my dress.

I smiled at my handiwork.

She wiped her face. "Bitch!" she snarled and pointed the blade at my face as she stepped in again. Grabbing a handful of my hair, she forced my head back and pressed the point to my throat. The raw fury reflected on her face coursed through my body like acid, burning away all logical thought.

"I was going to let my boys kill you while I claimed your husband's life, but I think it will be more painful for you to watch me drain him of all his humanity instead. I'm sure you'll see the sweet irony in all this when he is the one who strangles you to death."

Fuck you.

Her lips pressed together, and a snarl came from her throat. She stepped away and glanced at her minions. "Have at her boys. Make her suffer, but she needs to be alive and aware when he comes in here. He gets to do the honors, understand?"

They nodded and all their eyes turned to me, narrowing with evil undertones. The first punch hit where the bitch had stabbed me. Acute pain spiraled through me, and my knees gave out. I dropped to the floor, trying to shield myself from the next blow, but one man grabbed a handful of my hair and yanked me to my feet. My scalp screamed.

Alex's mumbling through the intercom paused the punch fest. I pulled in a breath of air, staring at his groggy form. His eyes blinked, and he glanced around the room, calling my name. Beverly, wearing the facade of me, gave me the most horrific grin.

"I want her to witness this." She waved towards the window. "And no toys. Not yet. I also don't want to hear a peep from this room, got it?"

I struggled to break the binding holding me in place and opened my mouth in a silent scream. The lack of ability to voice my distress bloomed a rage inside me that compounded when the bicorn stumbled out of the room.

Alex stopped yelling and just stared at her, blinking at the image of me with a bloody knife in my hand. He closed his eyes, and his sigh of relief came through the speakers.

I was so focused on him, I never saw the punch coming. One of the bicorn's minions sucker punched me in the side she had stabbed me again. Sharp pain shot from the wound, dropping me to my knees in a silent scream. Air locked in my chest as another grabbed a handful of my hair, lifting me back to my feet.

The agony was so acute that I missed what Alex had said to the thing on the other side of the mirror. The bicorn nodded and crossed the distance, dropping to its knees before Alex. It used the knife to cut the binds holding his ankles and one of his wrists before putting the weapon on the ground.

I squirmed, trying to get away from the next hit, but the struggle was useless. I needed to find a different strategy. I focused on the pain, using it to find the strength I needed. Using the leverage of the ropes, I executed a sidekick, connecting with Justin's groin as he stepped in to deliver another blow.

He went down hard, with an *oof*. The glare he sent gave me an indication that I was going to pay dearly for that, but before I could turn my attention back to the window, another punch yanked the air from my chest.

"What are you doing?" Alex raised his eyebrows and glanced at the mirror in front of him and then around the empty room. "Kylee," he said again, this time in more of a whispering growl I knew intimately.

The bicorn's hands slid up his chest as the filthy thing pressed its lips to his, stopping whatever argument he might have been launching. It was so very much like something I would do that I tilted my head back in a wail that should have broken the glass in the mirror. But only air rushed out of my mouth.

Justin slammed his fist into my cheek. I went down. My cheek flared as if someone had hit it with a blowtorch. Stars filled my vision. Again, one of the thugs grabbed my hair, pulling me to my feet. The scream in my scalp had gone numb. He pulled me far enough forward that I was bent over and my arms stretched at my side, straining both shoulders. The shit held my head back far enough, so the only thing filling my vision was the bicorn unbuttoning Alex's shirt. When it started kissing its way down his chest, I thought my brain would explode.

"Are you going to untie me so we can get the hell out of here?" Alex asked, but I knew that voice. That tone of we-shouldn't-be-doing-this-but-please-don't-stop filled my ears.

Another punch hit my side, lifting me off the ground. But it was nothing compared to the mental agony of seeing Alex succumb to the wicked monster. Tears welled in my eyes, blurring my vision, and my throat tightened.

The bicorn shook her head. A smile crawled across Alex's lips.

"Kinky," he whispered over the sound of his zipper being lowered. "Ah, fuck, Ky," he nearly groaned, and his head went back against the seat. His free hand slid into the nest of braids on the bicorn's head as he guided the pace of its strokes.

I hadn't realized Justin had lifted my dress until hands gripped my waist, pressing into the cut with the same force as his entry. My gaze was glued to the scene on the other side of the window. The soul-sucking bitch was deep throating him. Giving him the blow job I had called a rain check on at the hotel.

The asshole holding a handful of my hair leaned forward. "You are going to swallow me like that before this is over," he whispered in my ear before his teeth clamped down on the sensitive tissue. He laughed and tugged on my ear until warm liquid ran down my neck. He stood and delivered a blow to my side.

Justin pounded me with brute force, mimicking the fists hitting my torso. Each thrusting blow nearly tore my shoulders from their sockets.

Alex groaned, even as my violations continued. Alex's essence slowly seeped from his body with every vile stroke of the bicorn's mouth. His cheeks hollowed as his eyes rolled back with rapture.

Agony overwhelmed me all the way down to the cellular level. The cry forming in my soul vibrated in the back of my throat, and I forced out my dormant siren. The haunting melody escaped, filling the room. Hope and horror glimmered inside me.

The ecstasy etched in Alex's face disappeared. Wisps of his soul snapped back in place. His gaze shot to the glass, and swear it locked on mine, and I kept singing, damning him just as much as the soulless minions abusing me.

The only one in the vicinity with a soul heard my song, and it was going to be the death of me.

His gaze dropped to the thing sucking his dick. Shock skittered over his features. He moved faster than I imagined he could and had the knife from the floor embedded in the thing's throat before it could stop him.

He kicked it away from him and reached into his pocket. Relief swept over his face as he pulled the other dagger from his breast pocket. Once he cut through the binds, still holding his hand to the chair, he stood and zipped himself back up. Disgust weaved into his features, peeling his lips away from his teeth in a snarl as he glanced at the mirror.

My heart soared even with the pain wracking my entire form. I had no control over the bicorn's minions. They were too far gone to be influenced by my siren. My voice failed as another fist connected with my rib cage, piercing my lung with fragments of broken bone. I coughed blood. Fists continued to pound my body, bruising and breaking without hesitation. My shoulders screamed at the torque of an angle they had me in, and if Justin kept up the pounding pace he was at, both shoulders were going to dislocate.

The bang of the door being kicked off its hinges didn't stop the assault on me, although the one holding my hair let go and moved in front of me.

"It's your turn to swallow cock," he said, reaching for his zipper.

I caught the rage flash over Alex's face before the minion blocked my view of my doomed husband.

Before this soulless asshat could unzip his pants, fresh blood poured from him, drenching me. He fell to the floor in front of me, his throat sliced wide, almost to his spine. Alex's roar filled the space, even as Justin continued his assault, tightening his grip on my side to the point his fingers dug into my cut.

With a growl, Alex slammed the knife in the man's face to my right. The wet sound of him ripping the blade out of flesh followed. Before the man fell, Alex brought the blade across the distance to my left. Another rain of blood splashed over me. The maniacal fury in Alex's face caught my breath in my chest. He disappeared beyond my field of vision.

The hands gripping me ripped away from my skin, as did the brutal force pounding my insides to a pulp. A high-pitched scream filled the room, and it was shut off an instant later.

The rope around my right wrist snapped, and I fell, turning my head so I wouldn't break my nose on the floor. My cheek hit hard enough to create white stars in my vision. Then whatever binds holding my left wrist in place released. I lay still for a minute, trying to assess the overwhelming damage to my body.

"Kylee." Alex's soft voice pierced my mind.

I glanced up, wincing at the motion. Just moving my head hurt. I struggled to lift onto my elbows.

Alex crouched in front of me, his white shirt bloody from his carnage. I looked around me at the four dead men. My gaze landed on a dismembered penis, and I now understood what that high-pitched scream was for. A satisfied flush rushed through me at the twisted justice. The knife dripped thick red gore onto the floor near me. I slowly pushed myself into a kneeling position.

Alex handed me the knife, took off his tuxedo jacket, and put it over my shoulders as my teeth clicked against the shock, trying to overcome my body. His hand reached out and cupped my cheek.

"Your voice is beautiful," he whispered.

Tears flooded my vision and spilled over, creating hot paths down my cheeks. I had damned the man I loved. Silent sobs ripped through my battered body. He helped me to my feet before covering my mouth with his, trying to silence the violent shakes filling my form. His soul seared to mine, and despite the pain his grip on me caused, I melted into the kiss.

Both his hands gripped my cheeks tentatively, as if he thought I would crumble under his touch. The knife weighed down my right arm, and I didn't have the energy to lift it to return the sweet gesture.

His sudden inhale yanked the air out of my lungs in a painful pull. The kiss broke, and his wide gaze met mine before dropping to the hand still holding the knife.

A crease appeared between his eyes. "Ky…"

He sank to his knees and fell forward onto my legs. The dagger he had stuck in the bicorn's throat was now embedded in his back. Beyond him stood Beverly with a vicious smile. Alex had speared her throat, but he hadn't pierced her heart, which was the only way to kill a bicorn.

"Bitch, that soul was mine," Beverly hissed.

Rage encompassed me. With the flick of my wrist, the knife in my hand sailed true, carrying with it the power of my fury. I leaned forward, screaming my siren. The two-way mirror and all the glass in the vicinity shattered at the pitch of my voice.

The bicorn's smile faded. Her gaze fell to the ivory wood blade sunk to the hilt in her chest. She fell over backwards like a tree dropping. When her body hit the floor, the facade of Beverly disappeared, leaving the hideous, faceless creature in its place.

I fell to my knees next to Alex. His eyes focused for a fraction of a second, and then went dull. His spirit slammed into my body with the force of a hurricane, fusing to my cells, becoming a part of me, unlike those ancient doomed souls of my past who satiated my hunger and just disappeared like they never existed.

Alex was the only siren victim that melded with me like a new strand of DNA. I could feel him in my soul, which meant when I finally faced the music, Alex would be there with me, sharing in my torture. Sobs clenched my chest.

My siren self flared, letting loose a wail of sorrow that lingered in the air.

Chapter 12

I DIDN'T KNOW HOW long I lay with my head on Alex's shoulder. His shirt was paper thin and see through from my tears. My throat hurt from the siren screams, and every muscle felt as if I had gone through a meat grinder. I wrapped my hand around the hilt of the knife in his back and pulled. The strain ground the broken bones in my chest, and a whine escaped from the back of my throat.

I climbed unsteadily to my feet and tucked the knife back into the breast pocket of the tuxedo jacket I still wore. My bare feet crunched over the shattered glass as I crossed to the door, ignoring the symphony of pain each step produced.

I needed the ocean. Otherwise, I would die in this desert hellhole and drag Alex to hell with me. The memory of his warm embrace filled me, and my breath hitched. My vision blurred under a steady stream of tears as I stumbled outside.

A small parking lot circled around the vacant building, and only two cars sat in the lot. Even the windows of the automobiles were shattered. I approached the shiny black town car we had gotten into at the wedding venue last night, and my reflection came into focus. I let out a silent huff. I looked like a cross between the bride of Frankenstein and Carrie with the rat's nest that was my hair and the blood streaking my dress.

I tried the door handle, expecting resistance, but there wasn't any. I tumbled onto the glass-covered seat. The keys dangled from the ignition. I closed my eyes and turned the switch. The engine roared to life. The GPS system blinked on, and I typed in the Bellagio.

The directions said I was twenty minutes away from my destination. I leaned on the steering wheel, fighting another bout of tears. With the last of my energy, I put the car in gear and headed for the hotel with both my mind and body on autopilot.

I pulled into the valet service at the hotel's private entrance for gold customers, thankful we had booked a suite. Walking through the hotel lobby in the condition I was in would have scared the crap out of everyone. At least here, the number of people turning white and gasping was limited.

The hotel manager intercepted me halfway to the elevator.

"Miss Paradox?" he asked.

I tried to step around him, but the movement caused me to cringe in pain. I raised my left hand, showing him the rings.

"Mrs. Cervas," he corrected. "Are you hurt?"

I met his gaze, leveling my most serious stare, mentally telling him to get the fuck out of my way.

"Where is Mr. Cervas?" he asked, his voice dropping to almost a whisper.

My chin trembled, and this time I walked around him. I got to the elevator with no one else stopping me. In the room, I reached for the zipper and nearly fell to my knees at the motion. After a few tries, I pulled the knife out of the coat pocket and sliced through both sleeves, stepping out of the bloodied mess that had once been my stunning wedding gown. I crossed to the shower, still holding on to the ivory wood knife.

You need to get out of here. Alex's whisper filled my ears, but I ignored it.

I needed to feel clean, but even the spray of the shower hurt my bruised skin. Red flowed from my hair and my skin, but I forced myself to stand in place until all that flowed was a thin pink line from the stab wound in my stomach.

Drying off was another hellish nightmare, as was putting clothing on, but I did every necessary motion until I was dressed and my hair was combed free of knots. I glanced at the nightstand next to Alex's side of the bed. My car keys sat there, along with the valet ticket and a notepad with a scribbled note I hadn't seen before. I limped to the side of the bed and picked up the paper.

Just going to set up a few things and grab us some breakfast. I'll be back soon. Love you. A.

Tears burned my eyes. I folded the piece of paper and put it into my bag. I grabbed the car keys, rolled my suitcase into the living room, and sat on the couch, just staring at the photo album. With effort, I picked up the book and placed it into the suitcase.

Halfway to the door, I stopped and backtracked to the tuxedo coat crumpled on the floor next to the ruined gown. I squatted and rifled through the pockets, finding the photo instructions from the ceremony last night. Something about leaving that behind seemed as wrong as leaving Alex at that abandoned property.

I struggled to my feet and dropped the card in my purse. Numb to my injuries, I crossed back to the elevator and stared at the stains on the tile floor as it descended. I stepped out in the lobby to a flurry of activity, including a swarm of police. The manager pointed at me, and a couple of police officers crossed, blocking my path.

"Mrs. Cervas, we would like to take you to the local hospital," the female officer said. Her badge announced her as Detective Mills.

I stared at her and let go of the suitcase handle. *I just want to go home.* I signed and bit my lip, pushing down the rush of feelings clawing their way to the surface.

"We need to check you out." She reached for me. "You are still bleeding." Her voice was soft, and concern laced her eyes. Her hand landed on my shoulder, and I winced. "Please, ma'am. You are in shock. Let us help you."

I couldn't move my feet forward. Instead, I blinked at her and cocked my head, swallowing hard. I had to get to the ocean. My injuries were substantial enough that if I was brought to the emergency room here in Las Vegas, I would never leave.

I need my home. Please, just let me go. Tremors started in my chin, and my vision blurred. *Please. I can't stay here. I just... I can't.*

She followed my hands and glanced at her partner before meeting my gaze. "Can we just ask you a few questions before you go?"

I turned my glance toward the hotel manager and lifted the valet ticket. He nodded. I turned back to the police officers. Most of my brain was still in a fog, but something about Detective Mills's gaze made me sense sympathy.

Questions?

They traded a look. "Do you have any recollection of anything that happened to you this morning?"

I reached out for the handle of my suitcase to steady myself. A high-pitched whine filled my ears, and I gave her a slow nod.

"Then you know you are injured," she said.

How do you know?

"There were recordings," she said. "Recordings of everything," she added softly.

That seemed like a thing that bicorn bitch would do to tide her over between attacks. I glanced at the floor, my mind filling with a measure of trepidation. I used my siren, but I had no idea if it translated over to digital recordings. Good God, what had I done? I blinked and forced myself to meet Detective Mills's gaze.

"What do you remember?" Detective Mills asked.

I kept hold of the suitcase. *Everything,* I signed slowly and then moved away from them.

"What was that thing?" Detective Mills's partner blurted out.

I stopped. Because of my injuries, twisting around to face them wasn't an option, so I held up my hand and spelled out, *Monster.*

Silence resounded behind me. I limped towards the exit where my car sat behind the broken one I had left at the curb earlier.

"Mrs. Cervas, you need to be looked at. Please, at least let me take you down to the emergency room," Detective Mills said as she ran up beside me.

No. I can't stay here. I signed after the valet took my bag from me and stowed it in the trunk. *If you saw the videos, you know why.*

The detective tilted her head in sympathy.

He was my everything. Now, I need to go tell his children that he's dead. I can't do that from a hospital bed here.

The debate in the woman's eyes raged, and then she reached into her shirt pocket and handed me her card. "I really should take you to the hospital here," she muttered under her breath. "At least let me know you arrived home safe, okay?"

I glanced at the card. It had both an email and a phone number. I gave her a nod. She helped me into the car and shut the door. I pulled away, each turn of the wheel wrapping my midsection in a high state of anguish. The pressure I had to exert with my foot was a new hell that kept me alert.

By the time I pulled into my garage, I was ready to just plow through the back wall, keep driving down the beach, and let the water claim me. But Alex's narrative in my head kept me breathing, kept me as close to sane as possible. I turned off the car and closed the garage door.

It took me a few minutes to get the car door open. I swung my legs out and struggled to my feet. The moment I stepped away from the security of the vehicle, my knees buckled, and I collapsed onto the cold concrete.

Get your ass up, girl.

The strength of Alex's voice in my head jumpstarted my muscles. I pushed myself to my hands and knees. While I would have preferred to just stay on the concrete until my heart gave out from shock, I did not want to sentence Alex to an eternity of Lucifer's revenge.

I crawled to the door and pulled myself up. The pain almost loosened my siren, but I clamped my mouth closed and forced myself to walk towards my lifeblood. The ocean beckoned.

I had been in dire circumstances before, but I wasn't sure if I had ever been this close to death. The hundred yards of sand stretched before me seemed insurmountable, especially under the midday sun, leaving the sand scalding on my already scraped and cut bare feet.

Come on, honey, just a few more steps.

His soft whisper gently pushed me forward. I stumbled into the surf, dropping to my knees as a wave flowed over me. The water charge infused me, squeezing my form, turning every broken bone, every torn piece of flesh, and every bruise into liquid agony.

My blood sizzled in my veins, and if I had a voice, it would have been screaming as I writhed in the surf under the pure torment.

Healing had never been pleasant, but this... this was a whole different class of torture.

White spots dotted my vision. I attempted to crawl to the safety of the sand, but the water pulled at me, trying to claim my soul in the same manner I had claimed Alex's. Relentlessly rolling me under its will.

Darkness threatened, and I fought it as vehemently as I had fought all manners of creatures over the years.

Unfortunately, this was not a battle I was destined to win.

Chapter 13

SAND SCRAPED MY CHEEK. I lifted my head, blinking my eyes open. I didn't recognize the surrounding landscape. Instead of taking a closer inspection, I rolled onto my back, assessing my current condition. The clear night sky met my gaze. I blinked a few times, trying to bat the crust off my eyelashes.

I had stumbled to the water during the midafternoon. My brain couldn't grasp the idea that I had been tossed around in the surf for hours like an untethered skiff drifting at sea. It was a miracle this human form didn't drown.

I scanned the night sky and found the Big Dipper. It was low enough in the sky to be an hour or two after dusk. My house was close to a mile from this spot. I tentatively climbed to my feet.

Halfway home, the events of the day barreled back into my numb form and I stumbled, landing on my knees. A tidal wave would have been a kinder punishment. The sorrow scratched every surface of my skin while wrapping its elastic arms around my chest, squeezing until I couldn't draw a breath.

Tears burned my eyes, my throat, and cut warm paths down my sand-brushed cheeks. I had lost in the past, but not like this. Not to the point I had difficulty envisioning any kind of tomorrow.

If Alex wasn't riding shotgun with my soul, I probably would have gone suicidal.

Bullshit.

"Shut up." Only a whispered hiss of air came out between my lips. The water hadn't repaired my voice box, at least not to the degree I needed to be coherent.

No. I won't shut up. Not when you need a reality check. I will always be here, Ky. Always. His voice echoed in my head.

I wanted you by my side, not trapped in my head. Damn you. I told you not to come, I told him.

If I hadn't come, someone else would have died.

I opened my mouth to argue and snapped it shut. He was right. With the lack of time to really study the venues or the employees, I wouldn't have been able to narrow it down so quickly, and another couple would have paid the price.

I turned you into a murderer. My hands slowly formed the core of my sin, following the flow of my thoughts.

You did not. Seeing what those animals were doing to you... That did. His tone turned feral, and the exhale of a deep breath followed. His voice was calmer when he continued. *I would have gone psycho even without the influence of your voice.*

I stood and continued back to the house. The door to the garage was partially opened, and I couldn't remember if I closed it or not. I turned on the light, scanning the space. My gaze locked on the path of blood from the car to where I stood.

I shut the door, crossed to where the keys lay, swiped them off the floor, and popped the trunk. Pulling the suitcase out was much easier than carrying it down from the hotel room. I brought it inside.

The light on our answering machine blinked, but I ignored it. Instead, I pulled out the photo album and took a seat on the couch. My wet clothes squished against the leather, but I didn't care.

With my heart pounding in my throat, I opened to that first picture. The one where Alex wore the grin I loved. I ran my fingers over his face and bit my lower lip to stop the trembling. My ring shined in the overhead light. I closed the book. I couldn't go any further.

I had no idea how I would ever function normally with the pressure of his loss constricting my chest.

One breath at a time, babe. Just one breath at a time.

The End

Continue The Paradox Files with book three,

HUNTING THE SIREN.

About J.E. Taylor

J.E. Taylor is a USA Today bestselling author, a publisher, an editor, a manuscript formatter, a mother, a wife, a business analyst, and a Supernatural fangirl. Not necessarily in that order. She first sat down to seriously write in February of 2007 after her daughter asked:

"Mom, if you could do anything, what would you do?"

From that moment on, she hasn't looked back.

Besides being co-owner of Novel Concept Publishing, Ms. Taylor also moonlights as a Senior Editor of Allegory E-zine, an online venue for Science Fiction, Fantasy and Horror, and co-host of the popular YouTube talk show Spilling Ink.

She lives in New Hampshire with her husband and during the summer months enjoys her weekends on the shore in southern Maine.

Visit her at www.jetaylor75.com to check out her other titles and sign up for her newsletter for early previews of her upcoming books, release announcements, and special opportunities for free swag!

If you enjoyed WAKING THE SIREN, check out
the rest of the books in THE PARADOX FILES
series:

THE PARADOX FILES

**A protector. A lost soul. A siren looking for
salvation.**

Kylee Paradox never expected to be a protector of
humankind, but when hell's portals open and let
loose the creatures of the underworld, she can't
see any other way.

Armed with an ultimatum, Kylee has no choice
but to embrace her new position as bounty
hunter of the damned. Sending these monsters
back to purgatory becomes her life's mission.

The only glitches in an otherwise noble pursuit are those who hold her fate in their hands. They forbid her from using her deadly siren song to lure the beasts back to the pit.

If she harms even a single innocent soul in her quest, Kylee herself will become one of the hunted.

This set includes Silencing the Siren, Waking the Siren, and Hunting the Siren

You might also like THE RYAN CHRONICLES.

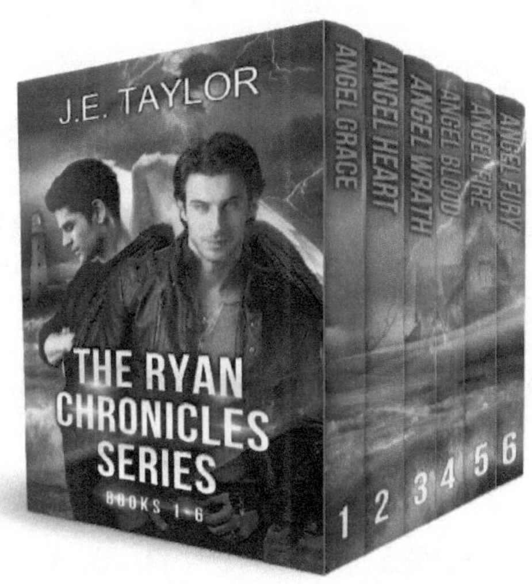

THE RYAN CHRONICLES

**Demons, vampires, angels, and the devil.
What the hell kind of nightmare do I live in?**

CJ Ryan was born with enough psychic power to destroy the earth. And Lucifer wants him to do just that.

Raised with a strong moral compass, CJ won't sacrifice innocent lives to protect his own, and that puts him at odds with the devil.

But if he doesn't give in, he and all he loves will become the target of Lucifer's rage.

When CJ gives his twin brother, Tom, a dose of
his powers to keep him safe, it puts Tom directly
in Lucifer's crosshairs.

As the final battle draws near, what will they
have to sacrifice to keep their loved ones safe?

Can they survive the devil's wrath?

THE RYAN CHRONICLES includes these titles:

CJ's Story:

ANGEL GRACE - Book 1

ANGEL HEART - Book 2

ANGEL WRATH – Book 3

Tom's Story:

ANGEL BLOOD - Book 4

ANGEL FIRE - Book 5

ANGEL FURY – Book 6

Fans of Supernatural and Shadowhunters will
enjoy this series.

Check out some of the other series set in the same world as THE PARADOX FILES.

FIRE CURSED TRILOGY

Lucifer's daughter rises.

Faith Kennedy's mother hid the awful truth from her daughter for sixteen years. Until she lay on her deathbed. Only then did she reveal who sired her daughter, and the revelation terrifies Faith.

The devil may have sired her, but he only wants her beating heart ripped out of her chest. After all, that's where her angel grace fueling her fire power is stored, and that will give him what he needs to bring about humanity's fall.

And Lucifer will take down anyone who gets in his way.

When Faith is given an ancient knife that can kill the devil, she faces the toughest challenge of her young life. She must hunt Lucifer and put him down. Otherwise, the world will burn.

But if she succeeds, she may wipe herself, and everyone she loves, out of existence.

This set includes Fire Cursed, Homecoming, and Judgement Day.

RUNNING FROM THE DEVIL TRILOGY

An escaped demon and a snarky cat face off against the seven deadly sins.

Escaping from Hell was just the beginning of Phoebe's problems. In Hell, she had a position of legend. A marquis of torture. But on the human plane, she is just another New York City destitute.

Before she has a chance to get her bearings on the unforgiving streets, Fate steps in and offers her a chance at redemption, but it doesn't come cheap.

She must bring in the demons that escaped alongside her while making sure no humans are harmed in the process. In order to do that, she needs to learn to live in the human world with the help of another one of Fate's parolees, a snarky cat named Smoke.

If it means never seeing the halls of Hell again, Phoebe will do anything, even battle the seven deadly sins single-handed.

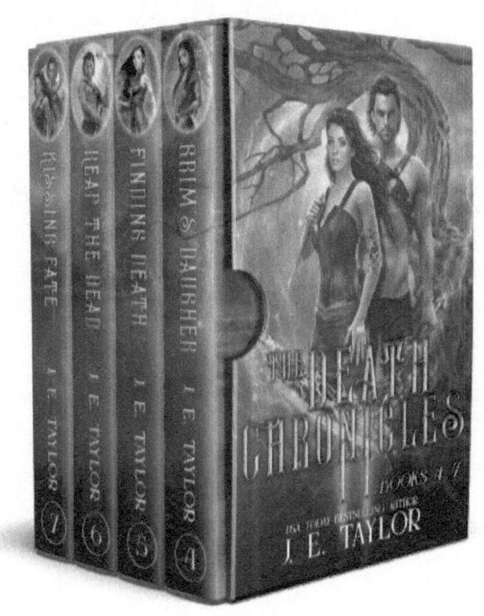

THE DEATH CHRONICLES II

Death is the family business, but not one I want to pursue. Thankfully, it's been passed down from father to son for generations, so it should skip me as Death's daughter. Then I won't have to stop being alive and can actually live my life. Right?

Well, the reapers don't agree. And neither do the angels.

One thinks I'm destined to take over, the other believes I will destroy existence. Both want me dead to match their own agendas.

I have an agenda of my own, and Leviathan who has sworn to protect me. But once my family and friends start being targeted, the family business, while grim, might be the only choice I have to save those I love.

The Death Chronicles *II* includes the following titles

Grim's Daughter

Finding Death

Reap the Dead

Kissing Fate

Check out some of J.E. Taylor's other fantasy titles:

SEASON OF THE DRAGON

Monsters, trust issues, betrayal, and a near death experience.

What else could go wrong?

The end of life as we knew it didn't come with a nuclear blast. It didn't come with the deadly impact of a hurdling asteroid. No. It came in a wave of illness that swept the world with fear, and in our quarantined silence, the monsters awoke.

Leviathans, serpent kings, and dragons came forth from the bowels of the Earth. The season of the dragon began with fire and fury and ended with a new world order. One in which these giant terrorists held all the power.

When Mikhail St. Clare betrays the monsters by saving me from death at their claws, I cannot trust the last remaining dragon shifter. Not when humankinds' survival is at stake, and he had a hand in our near extinction.

The only thing we seem to agree on is our desire to annihilate the leviathans and unseat the Serpent King. Our personal futures depend on ridding the earth of these murderous overlords.

We thought crossing the leviathan-patrolled city where every corner hides a hideous death was our most lethal hurdle. But building a bomb large enough to wipe out an entire species carries its own insane levels of danger.

One wrong move and we could destroy everyone living in New York instead.

THE FALLEN VALKYRIE DUET

A fallen Valkyrie. A Fae-Wraith hybrid.

Enemies become allies to survive a god's wrath.

Odin's Order to reap an innocent soul from Earth makes me question everything I have ever known as a Valkyrie. Protecting the innocent is our basis for existing, and now I must decide. Do I blindly follow his order?

If I don't, I will be just another casualty in Odin and Thor's destruction of the realms. Anyone who challenges their rule dies a very public death, regardless of their origins. And now they have enslaved Earth.

Reyfyre, a fae-wraith hybrid, and one of Asgard's enemies, has been hiding in this realm his entire life. When he finds me, he offers asylum as long as I help him kill Odin and Thor.

With everything they have done, how can I refuse?

When a bounty is placed on my head, we make the decision to leave Reyfyre's mountain sanctuary and head to New York to get lost in the city of millions. But the trek across the Canadian wilderness brings us face to face with hidden refugees, predators, and thieves.

There's no other option but to survive.

If we die, then there will be no one left to stop the callous gods before they destroy the only realm left.

But are we strong enough to take down a god?

If you like dark twists on Norse Mythology, you will love the Fallen Valkyrie duet.

SHADES OF NIGHT

The Monster Defense Agency demands loyalty and prohibits inter-agency relationships. And once you become an agent, the only way out is in a body bag.

When Sarah Stone and Robby Young train together at the agency's academy, sparks fly. And when they are paired as partners, they must muzzle their attraction, or they will face a firing squad.

All their pent-up frustration sharpens them into finely tuned monster hunters. Their ability to neutralize entire nests of vampires becomes the stuff of legends.

But hunting vampires has its own risks. Especially when Sarah and Robby uncover duplicity and corruption at the highest echelon within the Monster Defense Agency.

With a bull's-eye on their backs from both the agency and the vampires they hunt, Sarah and Robby's only hope is to take down the Monster Defense Agency.

But two against an ancient organization that trains monster-killers and knows all their tricks is even harder than it sounds. It's going to take all their skill and intelligence to kill this beast.

And being caught is not an option.

Shades of Night delivers forbidden mates, cool magic, and a kick-ass heroine in this fast-paced urban fantasy series.

Books included in this special edition hardcover:

Young Blood – A Shades of Night Prequel

Wicked Heart – Shades of Night Book 1

Crooked Soul – Shades of Night Book 2

Tainted Mind – Shades of Night Book 3

PACK MAGIC

She's a hybrid alpha scorned by her pack, until he arrives.

Daughter of a tribrid and a flame-touched alpha werewolf, Erica Young's course in life should be set. Except no one wants a phoenix-werewolf with a taste for blood to be their alpha.

When the head of the werewolf council shows up with a possible candidate to take her place in the pack, sparks fly.

Logan Blaez, the prodigal son of the council head, is willing to challenge Erica for the role of alpha, even if that means a fight to the death. Until he lays eyes on her.

Now he wants to claim Erica as his mate and rule as her alpha.

Too bad Erica isn't willing to submit, or give up her birthright.

THE WITCH ASSASSIN

An assassin tasked with taking out a mythical fae king...

In a realm that doesn't exist...

Mya's mission is to get in, obtain the fae king's DNA, and get out.

It should be easy with her gifts, except when does anything ever go as planned?

But failing in her line of work is a death sentence, and nothing in her training prepared her for Tavin Zorander—the most powerful Elvren to ever exist. After all, it's his family's magic that's kept his kingdom cloaked from the prying eyes of the universe for centuries.

When she finds herself at the mercy of the fae king, Mya has a choice to make.

Does she use her darkest power, thus compromising her mission, or should she surrender to Tavin's desires and put his entire kingdom at risk?

Find these titles and other fantasy, romance,
and suspense titles on J.E. Taylor's website!

www.JETaylor75.com